"I do not want to make you angry, Jessie."

A desperate tingle of anticipation ran through Jessie, looking at this big, troubled man who nonetheless retained a streak of tenderness.

"If I'm angry, it's not because you make me so," she replied. "Part of it's just that I was born that way. I can't help it, and neither can you, I suppose—even if you wanted to, James."

His hand tightened around her shoulder, and Jessie felt herself being pulled toward him. Jessie did not resist the tug of desire, but allowed it to happen...

→ **WESLEY ELLIS** →

LONE STAR

AND THE APACHE REVENGE

A JOVE BOOK

LONE STAR AND THE APACHE REVENGE

A Jove Book / published by arrangement with
the author

PRINTING HISTORY
Jove edition / May 1984

ISBN: 0-515-07533-7

Jove books are published by The Berkley Publishing Group,
200 Madison Avenue, New York, N.Y. 10016. The words
"A JOVE BOOK" and the "J" with sunburst are trademarks
belonging to Jove Publications, Inc.

PRINTED IN THE UNITED STATES OF AMERICA

Chapter 1

Their camp lay on the dry lip of the desert, two days' ride from the town of Las Cruces, to the west. It was past midnight. Jessica Starbuck and her companion, Ki, slept in their bedrolls, leaving Don Schaeffer to stand watch. It would be Ki's turn in two hours, before the party set out again at dawn. A cold breeze kicked down from the Sacramento Mountains to the east, and chilled the lone guard, who could see nothing and hear nothing in the silent moonless night.

Schaeffer was a trusted Circle Star hand, second in command to the ranch foreman, whom Jessie had wanted on this trip for his trail-toughness and his knowledge of cattle. It had been an exhausting ride so far: four full days in the saddle, covering increasingly difficult terrain on their way

1

from West Texas to New Mexico Territory. Schaeffer was as tired as his boss, and he fought the urge to close his eyes. He breathed in lungfuls of the frigid desert air and splashed a precious handful of water on his face. It helped some. He held his Winchester canted across his right shoulder as he crouched near a smooth rock. This was a land of rocks and dust, ringed by mountains and infested with scorpions and hostile Indians. Despite its deadly vastness under the sun during the day, it was not an empty land, and at night the creatures—men and animals—who lived here came to life. Soundlessly, the desert bloomed danger.

Don Schaeffer did not see the intruder until the man was upon him. A powerful hand locked around Schaeffer's mouth and muffled a shout. The ranch hand's rifle fell to the ground, and he grappled with the man in the dark.

As the gun clattered against a rock, Ki was out of his bedroll and on his bare feet. With a mountain cat's leap he was upon the intruder—a tall, muscular man. Jessie, too, was aroused from her light sleep, and she reached for the .38 Colt that lay beside her beneath the blanket. Without a word she moved toward the sound of the struggle, the Colt raised, searching through the darkness for a target.

Ki jumped on the big man's back and wrenched him away from Schaeffer. The guard scrambled free of the intruder's grasp and went to pick up his Winchester. Ki spun the man around and faced him, a shadow looming in the blackness, towering over the wiry Oriental.

Ki assumed a classic *te* fighting stance—his weight on his rear leg, his fists poised, his breathing even. As his eyes became more accustomed to the darkness, he judged his opponent to be about six and a half feet tall, dressed in soiled trail clothes, and wearing high-topped leather moccasins with beadwork. He carried no gun, but a bowie knife hung from his belt in a plain sheath. The stranger made no move, but looked around to locate Jessie and Schaeffer. He was caught off guard by Ki's sudden attack.

2

The samurai lunged into a low, sweeping kick and hooked his right foot around the stranger's knee, then yanked the leg forward. The man's knee buckled and he fell to the ground with a grunt. But, as Jessie watched, puzzled and afraid, the man sprang to his feet again and attacked Ki. Moving with the lithe grace of a trained fighter, the stranger reached out his long arms to collar Ki, who spun on one foot and delivered a high, snapping roundhouse kick to the man's chest. Unfazed, the man advanced again on Ki, blocking the samurai's fist-edge strikes.

Jessie held her Colt on the intruder as he dodged Ki's blows. Schaeffer, having recovered his weapon, had the man covered as well.

Expecting the stranger to pull his knife, Ki wanted to bring the man down before that could happen. The samurai had no weapon available, having sprung from his sleep wearing only his jeans. He drew back from his opponent and moved in a tight circle around him. The man moved like an Indian, his eyes—even in the heavy darkness of this night—locked on Ki's torso. The two men's feet shuffled in the dust; not a word had been spoken yet between them.

The man pulled Ki off balance with a flying tackle at knee height. The two went down, the bigger man on top, and Ki struggled to roll free of the man's weight. With all his strength, Ki levered the stranger off and slipped free, jumping to his feet and planting a heel at the man's throat. For a brief second the man did not react, then he clasped Ki's ankle with both powerful hands and, squeezing as if to crush the bones, twisted Ki's entire leg until the samurai toppled again to the earth.

"Ki!" Jessie cried.

Schaeffer jacked a cartridge into the chamber of his Winchester and brought the rifle stock to his shoulder.

Moving with amazing quickness for a man his size, the intruder pounced upon Ki, who lay stunned and fighting for his breath. Pinning the samurai by the shoulders, the big man hissed, "Do not talk. Do not shout. I am not your enemy."

With that, he released Ki and stood, his arms relaxed at his sides. He walked toward Jessie, who held her revolver aimed at his chest. Schaeffer moved to side Jessie as Ki rose from the dust. The man stopped five feet from Jessie's upraised gun.

"I come in peace. I did not mean to frighten you." He spoke in a near whisper. "We must not make noise. An Apache war party is camped no more than a mile from here." He pointed to the north. "They know you are here."

Ki came up behind the stranger. Impressed by the man's strength, he was nonetheless unconvinced that he was not their enemy. "Why did you sneak into our camp?"

"I could have killed you all if that had been my intention," the stranger said.

Jessie replied, "I don't think so. If Ki hadn't killed you, I would have finished you off. What do you want?" She held the .38 Colt steadily in position.

"I am sorry to have caused this disturbance. I have been following you for two days—and the Apaches have been on your trail, too. I wanted to warn you of their presence. That is all. I did not want to call out to your camp, because their scouts would have heard me. In fact, I am sure their entire camp is now awake, wondering at the woman's cry. They will be very curious. I suggest we leave this place immediately."

"Wait a minute," Jessie said. "We don't know who you are. Why should we believe you?" She glanced over at Ki, who stood relaxed but ready to confront the stranger again if necessary; she could tell that the man had won Ki's respect with his skilled fighting.

Beside her, Don Schaeffer said, "We've got him covered, Miss Jessie. You want we should tie him up?"

The stranger laughed softly. "You will not take me prisoner. You need me to help you fight the renegades. I am

4

telling you this for your own good."

"Come and sit with us, then," Jessie suggested. She lowered her revolver. Something inside her—instinct, trail sense—told her the man was speaking the truth. But she knew she mustn't let down her guard until she'd found out who he was and why he was here.

Ki nodded at Jessie from behind the big man. He agreed with her. He moved back to the cold camp and sat cross-legged upon his blanket, showing the man he had no fear, that he was willing to listen.

The big man hunkered down near the smooth rock where Schaeffer had been standing watch. Pointing at Schaeffer, he said, "I understand your caution, but I would prefer to speak without that man's rifle at my neck."

Jessie said, "I would prefer that he remain where he is." But she told Schaeffer, "Hold your gun down and don't shoot unless our guest moves too suddenly." Turning back to the intruder, she said simply, "We're listening."

"As I told you, I did not mean to bring trouble here— but only a warning. And to offer you my gun to help you fight these Apaches. They are a renegade war party, about twenty men. I would not like to see you wiped out in the desert. I have seen that happen too often."

Watching him, listening to his straightforward words, Jessie did not know what to make of this strange man from nowhere. She could make out the dark, chiseled features of his face: a hawklike nose, high cheekbones. He wore his hair nearly shoulder-length, with a kerchief tied around his head, very like the Apaches about whom he was warning them. His shoulders were immensely broad, his arms long and muscular, his hands large and unmoving. As he spoke he looked directly at Jessie with his black eyes, glancing occasionally toward Ki.

"This man," he said, indicating Ki, "is a strong fighter. I am honored to have fought him, but I wish to be a friend and fight alongside him instead. My name is James Camp-

5

bell. What is your name?" Ki told him. "And your name, ma'am?" The respectful form of address sounded strange, coming from this dark man's lips, for he looked as savage as the land from which he had come.

"I'm Jessica Starbuck," she said. "I'm on my way from my ranch in Texas to Las Cruces, on business. Where are you bound, Mr. Campbell?"

The man picked up a pinch of dust and let it fall through his fingers. "I am riding to Las Cruces, too. On business."

Jessie thought she detected a slight smile on the man's lips. She saw that Ki was watching the man, intently, sizing him up, measuring the threat he posed to the party of Texans. Ki met her gaze in unspoken agreement. He believed what this man Campbell said, and was inclined to trust him. If there were hostiles close by, they would need all the help they could get in fighting the Indians off.

"You are welcome to join us, Mr. Campbell," said Jessie. "But you said you were riding to Las Cruces. Where is your horse?"

Campbell gave a low, trilling whistle that was carried away by the wind. Within a minute, Jessie heard the approach of a horse. The animal appeared at the edge of the camp, causing the others' horses to snort and whicker in response. Campbell's animal went to its master and stood silently by, haughtily ignoring the greeting from its fellows. Jessie could make out the tall, well-built form of the horse; it looked to be a stallion, as dark brown as Campbell himself, with a white star on its forehead.

"We have water and feed for your horse, if you want it," Jessie offered.

James Campbell thanked her. "Yes, he needs water. He is a strong animal, but he has gone without water for a full day. It is not good to treat a fine horse like that."

Jessie realized that if his horse had gone without water, most likely Campbell had also. He did not appear to be the kind of man who would hoard water for himself at the

6

expense of such a beautiful, well-trained animal. He must have ridden hard and been unable to look for water. And with Apaches in the area, he had had to keep moving—or risk being caught flatfooted by the hostiles.

The stranger attended to his horse, then rejoined Jessie, Ki, and Schaeffer. The ranch hand now sat relaxed, his Winchester cradled in his arms. "I suggest we ride out within the hour," Campbell said, repeating his warning about the nearby war party. "This is no place to set up a defense."

Though Jessie was not at all comfortable taking orders from a stranger, she knew that what Campbell said made sense. It would be safer to move out now, rather than risk a predawn ambush. She took Ki aside.

"I'm inclined to go along with what he says," she told her samurai companion. She trusted Ki's judgment implicitly, and would not make a move if he disapproved.

"I believe this man Campbell is telling the truth," Ki said. "He is a strong warrior, and I think he is an honorable and truthful one. When we were fighting, he made no move toward that bowie knife he's carrying, and that tells us something important."

"I'm just thankful he wishes us no harm," Jessie said. "And if it comes to a fight with the hostiles, I'd rather have him on our side than against us."

Jessie told Schaeffer to saddle his horse, and she and Ki did the same, as Campbell waited patiently for the party to get organized. The ranch hand threw suspicious glances at the tall, dark-skinned man, and kept his Winchester close at hand until it was time to go. Finally, reluctantly, he slid the long-barreled rifle into its saddle boot as the four of them rode from the camp.

• • •

By the time the first pink glimmer of dawn appeared, they had ridden a good five miles—with no sign of the renegade war party. The fingers of sunlight began to stretch across the dry hardpan, illuminating the barren desert and framing the surrounding mountains in crimson and gold as the cloudless sky washed blue. Six hours later, there was still no sign of trouble.

James Campbell scouted ahead of the riders a quarter of a mile. Ki watched their backtrail with a sharp eye, ready to shout a warning if he saw any sign of the feared Apaches. Jessie and Schaeffer rode close together, and they, too, strained their senses to catch a possible warning of attack. Nothing.

As she rode toward Las Cruces with the others, tensed for any eventuality, Jessie Starbuck reconsidered the wisdom of this trip—especially her decision to go on horseback instead of by stage through this dangerous stretch of New Mexico, which had never been truly pacified by U.S. troops or anyone else. Her love of open country and her disdain for most means of travel other than horseback had prompted her to ignore the good advice she had gotten back at the Circle Star. She had been too long out of the saddle—buried in her father's old study in the spacious ranch house, poring through the books and ledgers, concentrating on business figures and reports from far-flung Starbuck operations, and tending to the dry, joyless aspects of a ranch operation. How many weeks had she spent at a desk, her fingers inkstained, her eyes glued to page after page of numbers?

It wasn't in her nature to sit still under any roof for too long. Having been raised by her father to ride and shoot as well as any man, Jessie felt more at home on a horse in the White Sands Desert than she did in a ball gown at a high-society function. In either situation, though, Jessie wouldn't fail to attract the eye of almost any man. Her lush coppery blond hair, startling green eyes, and astonishing figure were equally breathtaking in any setting.

And besides her itch to be in the saddle, she had some definite and potentially profitable business in Las Cruces.

8

Always looking for new markets in which to sell her Circle Star beef, she had been contacted by a cattle buyer who was offering good prices. Although she had firm markets already up north, in towns like Wichita and Kansas City, her vast cattle ranch was still growing. With the spring roundup concluded three months ago, she saw—in those same damned ledger books—that the Circle Star was likely to enjoy a surplus this year. If all went well—and one could never be absolutely certain in the cattle business—she stood to make some good money with this deal.

Jessie considered the challenge that lay ahead: negotiating the sale, bargaining over the terms and conditions, going head-to-head with an experienced businessman. That, too, was a part of her life as chief officer of Starbuck Enterprises, and she thrived on it. She was proud to match wits with men across polished tables in brass-and-leather business offices; her combative wit and intelligence had surprised and delighted more than one cigar-smoking tycoon.

She felt a ribbon of sweat trickle down her face as the hot morning wind raised clouds of alkali dust from the floor of the desert. Putting thoughts of business aside, she let her eyes sweep over the ragged landscape that shimmered in the intensifying heat-haze: in the distance, to the northwest, a dust devil danced evilly. Beneath the untroubled sky, the basin through which they rode seemed like a little corner of hell. Jessie wiped the dust film from her face and neck with her perspiration-soaked scarf.

Then Campbell rode back from his point-scouting position to join others. He waved for Ki to ride forward. Jessie felt a tingle of anticipation in her spine. It could mean only one thing—trouble.

When Ki caught up with the party, Campbell said, "Apaches up ahead. Probably the whole damn war party. I don't know how the hell they got there—must have swung around to the south. Now they're going to try to cut us off."

"Where are they?" Jessie asked.

"About a mile that way." Campbell pointed due west. A rocky red ridge rose from the barren earth and stretched for a half-mile across their trail. "They're behind that ridge. I saw the sign. Their ponies were headed in that direction. They must have ridden like hell for hours to beat us here."

Jessie thought she saw a glint of admiration and amusement in the strange man's black eyes. For the first time she noticed a jagged scar that ran from his left eye down his cheek, nearly to the jawline. It mingled with the other creases that scored his leathery skin, and now she realized that James Campbell had Indian blood in him. How much she didn't know, but he definitely had some. *Could he even be part Apache?* she wondered. How else could he sense the exact whereabouts of the renegade band? Was it even possible that he was leading her, along with Ki and Schaeffer, into an ambush? Unlikely, for he could have killed them all last night—or at least tried hard to kill them. Jessie asked a more important question:

"How can we get out of here alive?"

Campbell smiled grimly. "We can handle them, Miss Starbuck, if we do it on our own terms." He turned to Ki. "How good are you with those arrows?" He pointed to Ki's lacquered *ebira* quiver that rode, with his long bow, behind the cantle of his Texas saddle.

Ki said, "Very good." He was not boasting, just stating a fact. Having been trained as a samurai in all the arts of warfare, he was confident in his ability to deal death when it was necessary—with almost any kind of weapon. It was never a pleasant task, but it was a part of his way of life.

"That's nice to know," Campbell said. "We'll have enough firepower, then, if there aren't too many of them. I think we ought to ride right at that ridge for another half-mile—like we don't know they're there. Then," he added, reining his big horse around and pointing to the north side of the ridge, "we cut in that direction and run like hell for higher ground, try to gain an advantage on them. They'll be concentrated in the middle, probably, ready to shoot or to ride down after us. And they'll be expecting us to run the other way, out of the desert instead of farther into it."

Jessie looked to Ki. "I'll admit I don't have a better plan," she said.

Before Ki could answer, Schaeffer put in, "Hell, it's crazy to ride that way. What if they cut us off and we can't get out of the desert? We'll die of thirst in there—if we don't get shot to pieces before." A practical-thinking man— a cowboy rather than a soldier—Schaeffer didn't like to gamble against these odds, for his own sake as well as for his boss's. "Jesus Christ, Miss Jessie—pardon my language—it's crazy, is all."

Ki said, "The best tactic is always the unexpected one. Mr. Campbell is right. And if we can gain the higher ground, it will be to our advantage." He looked from Campbell back to Jessie. "We don't have much water, though. We'll be taking a chance."

"I don't see any other way," said Jessie. In her heart she knew that the risks were high. If there were any chance of outrunning the Apaches, she would be in favor of riding as fast as possible to the south and west. But now that the party had been spotted by the Indians, there could be only one outcome to this meeting.

The four of them dismounted and gave each horse a quarter of a canteen of water. The animals must be at full strength when they made the run for the ridge. There would be no time to water the horses until after the battle—if they survived. Then they all swung back into their saddles and spurred their mounts forward, to the west, riding straight at the ridge where the hostiles waited.

Despite deep misgivings, Jessie coaxed her mount, a strong-muscled roan, ahead. The animal, too, sensed the danger into which the party was riding, and it snorted and shook its head.

11

Ahead, the ridge—actually an elongated mesa that jutted from the ground almost vertically, providing a perfect position for whoever controlled it—loomed ominously. There was no sign of life there, no indication of the presence of their enemy. Yet somehow, Jessie thought to herself, the Apaches *had* to be there; in her gut she knew Campbell's assessment of their strategy was correct. As she rode past a lone stand of ocotillo, she thought of their aloneness out here. If, after all this, she and the others were still killed by the renegades, no one back home was ever likely to know what had happened.

But these thoughts occupied her mind only briefly, for the horses were eating up the distance, and the ridge was getting closer.

The hot wind did not let up, blowing clouds of dust across their path. As they neared the half-mile point, Campbell, who was in the lead, raised his hand and signaled that they should be prepared to veer in the planned direction. The three riders grouped themselves closely together, their mounts tense, their eyes on the ridge that concealed their fate. Then, dropping his upraised hand, Campbell planted his spurs in his stallion's flanks and galloped away. Jessie followed, urging her horse to its maximum speed. Behind her she heard Ki and Schaeffer do the same. In a roiling cloud of alkali, they made for the natural ramp that would take them to the top of the mesa.

Suddenly they heard a chilling shout in the near distance—an Apache war cry.

Bullets snapped around them as they galloped, heads down, knees dug into horseflesh. Then came the popping sound of the Indians' rifles, echoing their death message across the flat, open basin. Ki clung to his lanky gelding as it stretched full length, racing ahead, and the half-Japanese, half-American samurai felt the hot breath of the Apaches' bullets as they whistled past him. At this range, over three hundred yards, the Apaches were at a disadvan-

12

tage; Ki guessed they did not have the best long-range guns, and thus were peppering the fleeing party with everything they had. Luckily it was not enough.

Jessie, too, felt the blazing closeness of the slugs, but as she and the others pushed their mounts toward their goal, it became increasingly less likely that they would be hit. Still, she wanted to take no chances. With the desert dust caking her face, Jessie could barely see, so she followed Campbell's horse. The whine of bullets grew less desperate, the shouts of the Indians less fierce. Then she felt the ground rise under her and she knew they had reached the incline.

The horses clambered up the slope, moving in single file along the narrowing trail that led between upthrust rock faces. The lead horse, Campbell's, whickered as it reached the top. Campbell reined it around to await the others, and unsheathed his rifle, a well-cared-for Spencer Model 1867. The short-barreled carbine looked almost like a toy gun in his big hand. He waved the others up, while keeping an eye peeled for advancing Apaches.

When Jessie, Ki, and Schaeffer topped the ridge, they saw that Campbell's plan was a good one; they were on elevated ground, defensible from all directions, and the Indians were five hundred yards away, down the ridgeline, angrily regrouping.

Jessie's party dismounted, gathering their horses near a sheltering rock face and out of the line of fire. Then the three men and the woman hastily took positions to cover every possible avenue of attack—Jessie behind a boulder guarding the trail from which they had just come, Ki on the west side of the rise that sloped gently down into the desert, Campbell to the north, from which direction the hostiles were most likely to come, and Schaeffer posted on the north corner to cut off access from there or to back the others in case of attack from another direction.

Having loosed his quiver and bow from the saddle, Ki hunkered down behind an outcropping to prepare his weapon.

13

First he strung the ash bow with a fine gut string, creating just the right amount of tension in the bow to allow himself maximum range and accuracy. Then, placing the bow aside, he turned to the lacquered *ebira* quiver, from which he removed fifteen war arrows with narrow, straight shafts and steel heads sharpened to killing razor points. These arrows could, when shot from as far as seventy or so yards, pierce a grown man's torso and slice clean through out the other side. He had made the arrows himself during idle moments at the Circle Star.

Nocking an arrow, he tested the pull of the bow: it was fine and felt right. With the arrow ready, he ventured a look at the enemy position.

The renegade Apaches were clearly visible now as they advanced like ants across the flat, rock-strewn top of the mesa, dodging from cover to cover. Ki estimated that there were twenty of them. He called to Campbell, "How many do you see?"

The stranger's tally matched Ki's. "About twenty—and all of them angry as hornets at our trick. They'll be wanting a fight, for sure." Campbell's Spencer lay in front of him, loaded, with a handful of extra cartridges laid out on a bandanna for reloading. With a rifle such as his, Campbell would concentrate on closer-range action, hoping to pick off the Apaches' advance guard.

Jessie finished loading her Winchester .38-40 Model 73, which used the same caliber cartridge as her beloved Colt. The wind blew her red-gold hair back over her shoulders as she squinted to gain sight of the Indians in the heavy glare of the day. Tired, taut, her belly feeling the breakfast she had missed, Jessie sighted on one renegade at the war party's right flank. The long gun lay perfectly balanced in her hands, the polished stock at her shoulder. She waited for the Apache to move within comfortable range.

Schaeffer shifted his position, moving up between Campbell and Ki so as to gain a better line. He didn't want to miss this fight; he'd never shot a hostile before, and he wasn't going to let this chance pass him by. He opened fire first. Two quick shots felled a renegade darting between rocks. The man pulled up at the bullet's impact, twisted and crashed to the ground.

Chapter 2

Jessie paused to reload her Winchester. She had pumped off fifteen shots in rapid succession, and the barrel of the .38-40 was hot to the touch. Despite her rapid fire, she had managed to hit only one Apache. As she worked the cartridges in, she chastised herself for the waste of ammunition. Overhead, bullets whanged off the broken boulders that served her party as cover. Campbell and Schaeffer continued firing, the smoke from their weapons hanging heavily on the air. Jessie regained her shooting position and sighted on one of the Indians, a man less than fifty yards away. He wore a red headband and carried a long-barreled rifle. She took her time, aimed for his chest, and squeezed off the shot. Her heart skipped a beat as she saw the man go down.

Even in the heat of battle she experienced a twinge of disgust at the necessity for killing. But there was no time now to think of such things. She looked for another target.

Ki, meanwhile, carefully nocked another war arrow and, with one knee planted firmly on the ground, waited for his best shot. Already he had claimed one renegade's life and wounded another. The Apaches were fighting ferociously, sending lead at the embattled travelers, giving them no time to do anything but try to match the attackers shot for shot. Ki, though, had the patience he'd acquired through supreme self-discipline, following the precepts of *bushido*—the warrior's code—and even with the blood tide washing around him, he waited for the best opportunity as the others blasted away at the Indians.

Finally he saw his chance: a renegade shouldering up against a low-lying rock about sixty yards away across the mesa top. Ki lifted the bow, gauging the distance, allowing for the Indian's cover—he'd have to shoot high in order to send the arrow down behind the obstacle. He released the shaft in a tight, high arc, and as the bow twanged, he immediately reached for another arrow. He knew that he had aimed precisely and was not surprised to hear a shout from the enemy as the shaft hit home. He caught a glimpse of the man and saw the arrow buried in the left side of his chest, most likely having pierced the Apache's lung. Ki loosed another, this time on a more direct line, at a renegade reloading his rifle. The startled Indian took the arrow in his gut, dropping the gun and slumping over, dead.

Schaeffer shouted, "We're gonna whip 'em!" He was firing rapidly, spraying the enemy positions with lead, raising a cloud of gunsmoke.

"Stay down!" Jessie cried. She didn't want to see one of her men get hurt, and she didn't like Schaeffer's cocky attitude. She had to duck herself as a bullet chipped off a piece of rock near her face. However many Apaches they had killed, there were still a good number out there—and those remaining had to be angry, itching to even the score with the riders who had eluded their ambush.

Campbell watched the Circle Star ranch hand's stupid

display, then turned back to the task at hand. With his Spencer he picked off one of the Indians, who was trying to skirt around the defenders' left flank. He allowed the man to move out, waited for him to hit an open spot between the rocks, and squeezed off a single shot from the carbine. The Apache stood straight up as the bullet lifted off a part of his skull in a shower of pulpy gore. The renegade's rifle clattered to the ground; another Apache went for it. Campbell finished off the second man with a well-placed shot. This man fell too, in a growing pool of blood.

Turning to Jessie, Campbell called, "How are you doing with ammunition?"

Jessie replied, "Okay for now. We've killed at least eight of them."

"I count nine," Campbell said. The crash of rifle fire all around them made it difficult to communicate without shouting. The dark man called to Ki, "That's good work with the bow. Keep it up." He swung around again to face the enemy. There were ten or twelve more renegade warriors to deal with, as the battle dragged on.

Schaeffer grew more excited. He continued to blast away, hitting one of the Apaches in a blaze of bullets that chewed into the renegade's gut. The ranch hand whooped and raised a fist. "Come and get it, you red-bellies!"

He's catching the killing fever, thought Jessie. It sometimes happens that once a man gets his first taste of blood, he finds himself possessed with the hot greed for more; she had seen it happen to otherwise gentle, thoughtful men who, having once killed, simply had to have more. She didn't like to see it, especially in a trusted Circle Star employee.

She called out to Schaeffer, "Cool down, Don. Be careful!" She saw him stand up as he finished reloading, and start spraying the Apache ranks with lead as rapidly as he could.

Damn him, she cursed to herself. *He'll get himself—*

Then it happened. As he jacked another cartridge into

19

the chamber of his Winchester, Schaeffer took an Apache bullet in his gun arm. The rifle spun from his grasp and fell out of reach. Startled, the ranch hand looked around, not hearing Jessie and Campbell shout for him to get down.

Ki sprang into action, hoping to reach Schaeffer and pull him to the ground. But he was too late.

In a matter of a few seconds, Schaeffer was riddled with bullets. One smashed into his face just below his right eye; three other slugs penetrated his chest, one tearing right through his heart. Blood pumped from these gaping wounds as Schaeffer's head rolled. The air around him was buzzing with bullets, like bees attacking a roving bear. By the time Ki reached him, the ranch hand was a bleeding hulk, and he collapsed onto the ground among the dozens of brass casings from the bullets he had spent.

"Oh God!" Jessie cried, tears stinging her eyes. She wiped them quickly, so as not to lose sight of the enemy. She levered off two shots, catching one of the Apaches who had killed Schaeffer. Fighting a blinding rage, she tried to be careful, choosing her shots, not wasting lead. She glanced over at Campbell, who was doing the same.

Ki reached Schaeffer and knew there was nothing he could do. The dry earth absorbed the dead man's blood as it flowed from the several bullet holes. The body twitched for a few brief seconds, then lay still—a battered shell of flesh that would soon attract carrion birds. The same could happen to the rest of them, too, Ki realized, if they did not beat back the Indian attack. He resumed his position and took up his bow.

Now Jessie's ammunition was running low. Each shot had to count. She picked her targets with care, killing one renegade with three shots. Campbell, meanwhile, downed two more of the enemy. It was only their commanding position on the high ground above the ridge that gave them this advantage, she knew. If their positions had been reversed—if the Apaches were up here and her party below—

Schaeffer would not be the only one of them dead by this time. Aggressive, skilled fighters, the Apaches were hanging on, even though they'd lost more than half of their number. But it couldn't last, Jessie knew. There had to come a point—and soon—when they would withdraw to regroup. She swung her Winchester toward a man who stood, making an excellent target, forty yards away. She fired, felt the kick of the rifle, and saw the man crumple in a heap.

Some of the remaining renegades let out a shrill war whoop. They increased their fire on the beleaguered defenders. Ki eliminated another Apache with a perfectly placed war arrow that sliced through the man's neck. Campbell blasted away with his carbine, trying to keep the enemy from advancing any further and keeping an eye out for any that strayed from the main body to launch an assault on either flank.

Jessie inhaled the pungent smells of hot metal and gunpowder. Again she reloaded, scooping up the last dozen cartridges she had. Overhead, the relentless sun burned down upon her, causing perspiration to wash down her face and arms. Thirsty, tired, racked with grief at Schaeffer's death, she fought on.

Ki saw Jessie's condition. It was his sworn duty to protect this beautiful young woman whose father had been like a father to him, as well. He released another shaft that sped up and across the burning blue sky, arcing down upon an unsuspecting warrior, who took the arrow in his clavicle. The sharp steel arrowhead sliced into the man's upper body, paralyzing him and then rendering him lifeless.

Reduced in number now to a handful, the renegade war party began to pull back. Strewn across the flattened ridgeline were more than a dozen bodies. Their shots rang and echoed as they covered their retreat. Then, as suddenly as they had appeared, the Apaches were gone. The exhausted party of travelers watched and listened as the Indians made

21

for their horses, gathering the riderless animals with their own and thundering away down the steep slope. A plume of dust rose as they hit the desert, then turned northwest and galloped off toward their mountain hideout.

Jessie stood, dazed, her face streaked with dust and sweat, her stomach hollow. "Dear God," she gasped as she went over to Don Schaeffer's bloodied corpse. She knelt beside him for a moment, then shut her eyes and turned away.

As if reading her thoughts, Ki came to her and put his strong, slender arm around her shoulders. He saw the tears mingling with the grime of battle on her face, below her red-rimmed eyes. "Do not blame yourself," he said. "Schaeffer brought death upon himself. He was careless— just for a moment, but long enough to die for it. You are not at fault, Jessie."

Campbell said, "Your friend is right, Miss Jessie. Don't go blaming yourself. We'll have to bury him quick and get moving again—out of this damned desert." He looked up at the sun, felt its unforgiving force. "I don't want to make camp anyplace near here."

"I'll help you bury Schaeffer," Ki volunteered. He went for the small shovel he always carried. When he returned with it, he and Campbell dug the grave right on the spot where Don Schaeffer had fallen.

It was well past noon by the time they buried him, filling in the grave with loose dirt and rolling several stones over the site to keep scavenging desert birds and animals away. Then, without ceremony, Jessie and the others went for their horses and mounted, riding away without looking back.

• • •

By nightfall they had made ten long miles and kept going for two more hours before stopping, finally, at a spring to which James Campbell had led them. He seemed to know this part of the country as well as any Apache. Jessie continued to wonder at this, but kept silent during the ride.

They unsaddled and watered their horses, and the animals drank greedily from the spring. Then the riders filled their canteens and tasted the fresh, cool water themselves. Campbell gathered kindling and a few sticks of dry greasewood and built a small, smokeless fire in a low bed ringed by rocks. Though a fire was chancey, he and the others were eager for a hot meal.

Jessie prepared coffee, scalding it thoroughly, and served it to the men in tin cups. She put a cup of coffee to her lips and drank some down and felt the bitter liquid burn her stomach. Then she sliced up a hunk of cured beef in a pan, added a bit of water and chunks of wild onion, and set it on the fire to simmer.

She sat back, leaning against her saddle, and saw Campbell looking at her. "I'm sure glad we ran into you, Mr. Campbell—or that you ran into us."

The dark man nodded. "I'm glad there was no killing last night—there was enough of that today."

Jessie sipped her coffee. "I'd give anything to have Don Schaeffer here with us instead of lying on that ridge," she said softly.

"He will feel no more pain, know no more hunger and thirst," said Ki. "He is safe now with his karma. He was meant to die today. That is all."

"That's true, I suppose, but what is this thing called karma?" asked James Campbell.

"A man's life force, his fate, his past and his future—all of this is his karma. It was good karma that you did not kill me last night," Ki added. "Or that I didn't kill you."

Campbell gave out a low laugh. "I see what you mean."

"You say you're riding to Las Cruces too?" Jessie said, stirring the stew. She then sliced open a can of beans and mixed them in the pan, adding a pinch of salt from a small sack she carried.

Campbell said, "Yes." He put down his coffee cup and

23

moved closer to the fire. He gazed intently at Jessie, her finely sculpted features apparent even through the film of dust and grit on her face.

So hungry had she been that she had not taken time to wash her face, and she was embarrassed now that she hadn't. Whoever this strange man was, she felt powerfully drawn to him—grateful, of course, for his help in fighting off the renegade Apaches, and something more that she could not quite figure out. She served up the meal, which both Campbell and Ki wolfed down, topping it off with more coffee. Jessie took only a small portion for herself, hungry yet unable to eat very much. Each bite of the delicious meat and gravy was a strain. It was Campbell's presence, she decided, that had her so unbalanced.

When they had eaten, Campbell sat back, pulled a pouch of makings from his pocket, and tapped out tobacco on a small piece of wheat-colored paper. He rolled a fat quirly and licked it securely together. Igniting it with a stick from the dying campfire, he drew on the cigarette. The tip glowed red and he exhaled the smoke, as he gazed up quietly into the black night sky. As Jessie gathered the plates and pushed the coals of the fire under the dirt, she again felt the power of his presence; he was, she sensed, a lonely, troubled man, and she aimed to find out more about him.

At the spring, Jessie washed her face and hands and wished to God she could have a hot bath. In the distance a coyote howled, and a chill threaded up her spine as she thought of the bloodshed earlier in the day. She cleaned herself and her cooking utensils as best she could.

Ki agreed to take the first watch, and he moved out from the camp a short distance to take a look around the immediate area. Jessie repacked her cooking equipment. Although she was ready to sleep, she wanted to talk to the stranger, and this was the first chance she had had to do so.

She sat across from Campbell near the bed of dead and

dying coals from the fire. Tonight a sliver of moon was visible, and it cast a faint, eerie light upon the campsite.

Jessie was surprised when Campbell spoke first.

"The meal was good," he said. "I was hungry."

"Ki and I were hungry, too. I'm glad you liked it."

In the long moments of silence that followed, Jessie tried to frame her question in such a way that he would not take offense. In the end she simply blurted, "Who are you, Mr. Campbell? If you don't mind my asking, I mean. If we're going to be riding to Las Cruces together, I'd like to know." She waited, tensed for his reply.

Campbell said, with the slightest tinge of self-mockery, "To the whites I am a half-breed or, worse, a plain goddamned Injun. To my people, whom you call the Comanche, I am a warrior." The big man shifted his feet under himself, holding his head high. In the weak moonlight, the chiseled contours of his troubled face were apparent.

"My mother, Wandering Star, was daughter to a war chief. My father, Arthur Campbell, was son of a wealthy sea merchant; he was from Boston in Massachusetts. Have you ever been to Boston?"

"A few times," said Jessie. "It's a beautiful city."

She thought Campbell smiled as he said, "Beautiful to some, perhaps. I spent a year there." He paused and gathered the makings for another cigarette.

Jessie watched the shadowed figure with the broad, powerful shoulders as he poured tobacco from the pouch into the paper. The gesture was easy and sure, yet Campbell seemed to be quelling a stormy battle raging within himself. He lit the quirly with a glowing ember, then once again lifted his face toward the sky.

"I want to know all about you," Jessie said quietly, unsure of the effect her words would have on this taciturn man. She trusted him now, after the danger they'd been through together, yet there was something more, a feeling that had not defined itself. She wanted to know more.

25

"I have told you the important thing—who my mother and father were. I came from them, and now they are no more. I do not know for certain who I am anymore, and I do not know what to tell you."

"Where did you grow up?"

Campbell rocked back on his folded legs. "I grew into manhood with my people. I grew up beneath the big sky and among the buffalo and with the women who swept clean the floors of our lodges and with the men who taught me bravery. I grew up in the days when my people's medicine was strong and there were no soldiers killing our women. I remember so much—and yet I am not a storyteller, not like my grandfather was. My grandfather was Gray Wolf, who had counted many coups and led many men in battle and stole many horses from his enemies. He could tell tales in council that made my blood run like an icy river. In those days I was called by a different name; the name he gave me was Two Wolves."

Jessie remembered the stories her father, Alex Starbuck, had told her about the Comanche and Kiowa raids on white settlers in West Texas. The Comanche were an especially warlike tribe, cruel to their enemies, lightning-fast on their horses, unrelenting in their pursuit of battle. But as her father described them, they were generally a muscular, short-legged people—and some of their leaders tended toward fat from eating too much and too well. The man sitting near her was indeed muscular, but incredibly tall. His father must have been a very tall, long-limbed man, for these were not Comanche traits.

"Grandfather named me for the two wolves that appeared outside our lodge on the night I was born," Campbell continued. "He took this as a sign—a good sign. The wolf is powerful medicine, and two are twice as powerful. Since I am the son of two peoples, attended in birth by two wolves, my medicine must be doubly great." The big man laughed ironically. But he sounded unaccustomed to much laughter.

26

"Gray Wolf was a great fighter, but not a prophet. If he could see me now, he would know how wrong he was. Being of two peoples brings nothing but trouble."

"How long have you been away from the Comanches, your mother's people?" Jessie asked.

"For twelve years. I lived with her people for eighteen years, hunting and fighting and learning the ways of the land. My father died when I was ten—of smallpox, which killed hundreds of Comanche, as was intended. He had given up his own people to live with the Comanche. It was not easy for him. I know now how he felt, trying to live in a different world. But he loved my mother and they would not be parted. She mourned him for a long time, and she never remarried, though many chiefs and sons of chiefs wooed her. She raised me, along with Gray Wolf, and soon I had stolen my first ponies and counted my first coup and I was on the way to manhood."

Campbell paused. Not only was he unused to speaking so much at one stretch, but the words themselves seemed painful to him. Jessie waited quietly, without saying anything, fascinated by his story. She could see, as he spoke, the Comanche village on the plains, the men riding out to hunt buffalo, the women and children working and playing among the lodges. His story pulled at her heart and she felt . . . not exactly sorry for him, but sad somehow.

He went on, the words coming more easily now with her sympathetic ear. "My father's people, from Boston, discovered where I was and sent the American soldiers out to bring me back to their fort, Fort Sill. One day the soldiers came to our village. I had been wounded in a battle with our Apache enemy and lay in my mother's lodge. Most of the men were out hunting. The soldiers killed many of the women and children, as well as some of the old men, and took me away. I could not escape because of my wound. They carried me to Fort Sill, where my father's brother was. His name was Douglas Campbell and he was a rich man.

27

He rewarded the soldiers well, and had me taken to the train, where a white doctor waited. On the trip to Boston I was weak, but the doctor helped me and cured my wound. By the time I reached the city I was recovered, but I did not know how to get back to my mother's people, who had been put on a reservation, those who survived the raid.

"It was strange for me, a Comanche, living in Boston with my uncle, and his wife, my Aunt Clarissa. They lived in a large house with servants and many rooms. They ate strange food—which I had to eat, too. As soon as I arrived, my aunt began teaching me to read and write. She recited from the Bible, and made me write down what she said, and then read the words in the book for myself. Have you ever read the Bible?"

"Yes," Jessie said. "My mother read it to me when I was a very little girl. And later I read it sometimes myself."

"It is a magic book, Christians believe. My aunt tried to make me one of them. She did not understand the religion of my people and called it pagan—which to her was a very bad thing. She told me of a place called hell, where all the unbelievers, like the Comanche, would go after death and suffer the fires of punishment for their sins. I told her my people were suffering already the fires brought by the soldiers, along with death and disease in the villages and the killing off of the buffalo. She told me this was her God's just punishment, but I could never understand why my people had to be punished." Campbell finished his cigarette and tossed it into the ashes of the campfire. He shook his head. "My aunt and uncle had never seen how we lived out here, away from their cities and towns. They believed only in their own ways and tried hard to convert me. All I could think of, though, was escape. I longed to be back with my people, but didn't know how to get there."

Jessie asked, "How long did you live in Boston?"

"I lived with them for a year, and then they put me in a school to learn more of the white man's ways. All I saw in

Boston were white faces, except for a few black men who were servants. Even when I sat in their church and listened to the minister preach about brotherly love, I felt the hostile eyes of the white people. They all hated me for some reason; they did not consider me a brother worthy of their Christian love. Even at the school, among young men of my own age, I did not fit in. They were more like boys than men, with their pale, sickly faces and soft white hands, wearing bows around their necks and tight coats that stank when they sweated. I was forced to wear the same clothes, but I bathed often, unlike them."

Jessie listened to the strange rhythm of Campbell's words. He blended the Indian cadences with the vocabulary of his white relatives. He saw both the humor and the injustice in his experience, and she liked that. Even while he acknowledged the whites' hypocrisy, he did not hate them for what they did. He was curious more than he was bitter—for he did not understand how men could say one thing and do another; that was not how he had been brought up by the Comanche.

"There was one white man, a professor, who became my friend. His name was Dr. Gerald Tynan. He often invited me to his home to talk about my life with my mother's people. Sometimes he wrote down the things I said. He told me he would like to write a book about my experience. I know nothing about writing books, but I kept going back to his house to talk to him—and to see his daughter. Her name was Diana." He looked up into the black sky, almost as if expecting the girl's namesake, the ancient huntress, to appear before him.

"What was she like?" Jessie would not let him end his fascinating story.

"I was a young man not yet twenty years old. But to me she was the most beautiful girl I had ever seen. Her hair was the color of the brightest yellow warpaint, her skin as white as the snow in the mountains. And I remember her

29

eyes—dark brown like the buffalo's. I told her that once and she almost cried. I think she did not like being compared to a buffalo!"

Jessie did not reply, but enjoyed the joke. She could tell that Campbell enjoyed the telling as well. His voice, even though he spoke quietly, was animated.

"The professor did not mind that I saw his daughter, but others in the school did. I do not even know how they found out, for I met Diana in Dr. Tynan's house. We never saw each other outside. Nevertheless—" He paused and Jessie could see his dark eyes drawn to hers.

"You see, they taught me some of the white man's big words. My uncle and aunt, and the professor, began to get threatening letters. The cowards were afraid I was 'corrupting' the girl, turning her into a savage, they said. In my classes I felt their hateful stares. So one day I decided to leave. Diana had saved some money, which she gave me, and I bought a ticket on the train. She helped me figure out my route, and one day she and the professor took me to the railroad station. In five days I was in Kansas City, and I have never been back to Boston. Don't intend to go."

"Have you ever told anyone this story before?" Jessie asked.

His white teeth flashed briefly as he said, "No. No one asked. Soon after that, I joined the army as a scout. I spoke well and I needed to live somehow. The pay was good— and I had learned the value of money. I joined up at Fort Riley, Kansas, and they sent me out to General Crook's unit in Arizona. Quite a man, that Crook. His superiors in Washington never appreciated him, but his men did. He took a special interest in me when he found out who I was. He did talk to me once—like we are talking now.

"He told me then, 'Son, it doesn't matter one confounded ounce where a man comes from, or the color of his skin. It's where he's going that counts a pound.'

"His officers, most of them, were good, too. So I wound

30

up fighting the Apaches down in Arizona, mostly near the Mexican border. Victorio, Cochise, even old Geronimo. Crook fought hard but clean, unlike most of the white generals. He didn't want glory—he wanted peace." Campbell paused, and silence descended. "I've been talking too much," he said finally. "That's not good. We need sleep. I will be taking the next watch."

"I wanted to talk to you," said Jessie. "It's really none of my business—but I was curious about you. I mean, the way we met and all." What she wasn't saying was that she had met many men in her travels in the West, but none of them had disturbed her and fascinated her as much in so short a time as this man, James Two Wolves Campbell. "You said you were riding to Las Cruces on business," she added.

The torrent of words, unusual for Campbell, had apparently dried up, and the coolness of the air now bit into them both. A night breeze whirled into the camp.

"I aim to set right a wrong," the half-breed said. "My mother, and others of my people, have died wrongly, without honor. Their deaths must be avenged."

"Who is responsible for their deaths?" Jessie asked.

"A man named Lowell Henry. I am going to kill him."

Chapter 3

Jessie asked James Two Wolves Campbell to explain. After all, what he proposed to do was murder—which she couldn't allow, no matter what the provocation.

Campbell told her succinctly. "This man called Henry got his dirty hands on a government shipment of beef bound for the reservation where my mother and her people lived. He switched the meat, sending rotten meat to the reservation and keeping the clean meat. Fifty people died from the disease carried by the meat. For that, Henry himself will die."

Jessie watched the lanky man as he shifted his legs, tossing the remains of the cigarette into the dying fire. She realized she had pushed him perhaps a bit too far. He had told her more than he intended, and more than she wanted to know. Still, there was no going back now. She understood this man's thinking, saw the justice in it—if, in fact, Lowell Henry was responsible for the terrible misdeed. But Campbell could get himself killed in attempting to kill Henry.

"What about taking this man Henry to court?" she suggested, though she knew very well how futile the suggestion was.

Campbell didn't hesitate to answer. "The white man's law is made for the white man. No judge or jury would punish Henry for this—not for killing Indians. You are not a stupid woman, you should know this."

"Of course I do, but—"

He raised a long-fingered, callused hand. "My word in a court of so-called law is worth as much as a grain of desert sand. Henry is a rich man with friends who are lawyers and judges. With his money he can *buy* justice. For me and my people, there is only one way to get justice."

"But you're part white, too. That should count for something," she pointed out.

"I have learned that it counts for *nothing*. That is what I learned from the white Christians who call themselves Americans. I have learned to hate their laws, because they themselves do not respect law."

Jessie bit her lip. The man that James Campbell wanted to kill was the man she intended to do business with. She wanted to tell Campbell, but could not. Not now. So she held her peace.

She moved closer to him. Despite the desert chill, she felt very warm and wanted to reach out to this man. Beneath the bitterness and violence in him, there was a vulnerability, a loneliness that she wanted to touch. There were no words for it, but the feeling was there—and somehow she knew Campbell felt the same way.

"I understand what you are saying," Jessie murmured, "but there has to be an end to the killing. Sometime there has to be an end."

"Not while I am still alive," said Campbell. "Not while Henry is still alive."

"If that's how it has to be..."

34

How could she convince this man otherwise? He belonged to two worlds—neither of which was totally his, neither of which totally accepted him for what he was.

"Let us not talk of it," he said quietly. He turned to face Jessie. "Nothing we say will change what I must do."

A deep longing welled up inside Jessie. James Campbell might be dead in a day or two, the way he was going. As he said, talk couldn't change that. But how could she reach him, make him know that he had something to live for? She touched his arm, looking directly into his eyes. Campbell said, "You are a beautiful woman. You have chosen to live differently than most women of your race. You should be home, married, bearing children for a rich white rancher. Why are you out on the trail, riding to Las Cruces?" The slightest trace of a smile curved his lips. He was goading her in his own subtle way.

Jessie threw her head back, color rising in her cheeks. She was glad the darkness concealed her blushing. "I have a great responsibility—something most women do not have. There is too much for me to do—my father's ranch, the business—I don't know if I'll ever get married. And besides, there's the matter of my father's death. Perhaps you've heard of him; his name was Alex Starbuck."

The half-breed nodded. "I have heard of your father. He was much feared and respected. He was murdered, I heard. I am sorry for you." His dark eyes sparkled in the last tongue of flame from the campfire. "So you have decided to avenge his death, is that it?"

"Part of it," Jessie acknowledged. "There were men— a conspiracy of businessmen jealous of my father's great success—who plotted to assassinate him. They are little men, cowards who hated him for doing what they could not. Yes, I seek their deaths if I ever run into them—which I do, much too often."

"I saw today that you are a woman who is capable of killing when she has to."

"I am my father's daughter!" Jessie blazed. "I can handle a gun when I have to, yes."

"You do better than just 'handle a gun,'" said Campbell. "You are damned good with one."

The burning in Jessie's face subsided a bit as she realized the half-breed was needling her, probing her defenses. Stepping back from the edge of anger, she said, "Thanks. I see your point."

"We are all willing and able to kill when it comes to defending the people we love," he stated, a strange sentiment coming from this rugged, rawhide-tough man. But it seemed a most natural, true thing as he said it.

Jessie saw exactly what he meant. "I thought we weren't going to talk anymore about killing." Her pouting lips formed a dark smile.

Campbell nodded. He reached out and put a large hand on her slender shoulder. "I do not want to make you angry, Jessie." It was the first time he had called her by her first name.

A desperate tingle of anticipation ran through Jessie, looking at this big, troubled man who nonetheless retained a streak of tenderness.

"If I'm angry, it's not because you make me so," she replied. "Part of it's just that I was born that way. I can't help it, and neither can you, I suppose—even if you wanted to, James."

His hand tightened around her shoulder, and Jessie felt herself being pulled toward him. She did not resist the tug of desire, but allowed it to happen. Then, suddenly, she was kissing him, this strange dark man with whom she and Ki had fought and ridden today—this man who had, in fact, saved their lives by warning them of the renegade Apaches. Now all thought of fear and bloodshed melted away as their lips met, crushing together hotly.

Jessie slipped her arms around Campbell, clutching him to her. She ran her hands down his muscled back, feeling the taut strength there, pulling him closer. His arms enveloped her, in turn, in a powerful embrace, and her breasts crushed against his rock-hard chest. They kissed long and lovingly, his tongue darting between her lips, exploring the depths of her open mouth. Hungrily, Jessie pushed her own tongue against his, eager to taste him.

Finally she had to beg for release to catch her breath and recover her balance. The stars above them were dancing dizzily as she looked up into the night sky and felt the muscular, bearlike arms cradling her like a child.

"Oh God, James," she whispered. She put her head on his chest, seeking shelter there from the storm that raged within her. Campbell stroked her luxuriant, fragrant hair. "I don't know why, but being close to you makes me feel sad. I don't even know you—except for what you've told me tonight. Still . . ."

"Don't say it, woman. We can't hope to explain what goes on inside us—our spirits govern themselves and do not always obey our commands." He pulled her head back and planted another kiss on her willing lips. "This is better than a fire to warm a man."

She listened for a moment, straining to hear a sound from Ki, standing watch, but she could not. She and Campbell were safe for a while here at the campsite.

Looking up into his eyes, Jessie fingered the top button of his shirt, then released it. The second and third buttons came open, and another, until finally his shirt fell open and she ran her hand over his chest—the hard, hairless, smooth surface ridged with muscle. Her fingers lingered over the dark nipples, teasing him. Then she bent and took one of his nipples between her teeth and bit lightly. He pushed her away and she smiled.

It must have been a long time since he's had a woman, Jessie thought.

His hands began exploring her body, strangely gentle for a man accustomed to a rough life. Jessie hastily unfastened her own blouse and let it slip from her shoulders; her breasts fell free and open to his touch. She heard him catch his breath as, in the darkness, he felt their perfect, soft roundness and caressed them. His hands sent wonderful sensations through her as he cupped her breasts and brushed over her distended nipples with his fingers. She thrust her shoulders back and closed her eyes to enjoy the agonizingly pleasant feeling. Then he bent his head and flicked his tongue over one nipple and then the other, repaying her teasing with some of his own.

Jessie ran her fingers through his long black hair, tracing the curve of his skull, holding him there at her breasts. With his tongue and teeth he covered every tingling inch of her outthrust breasts and she didn't want him to stop. But a deeper urgency grew within her and she lifted his head to kiss him once more. Campbell's moist lips burned against hers as she pulled his shirt off and reached down for his belt buckle.

He stopped her. "Wait," he said. He got up and brought back his blanket, which he laid out on the hard ground. "Come," Campbell commanded her, easing her down beside him on the blanket.

She did not even notice the unyielding earth beneath her, but only the long, lean body of the man beside her. Once again she went to work on his belt, as Campbell held her and kissed her long, velvety neck. When the buckle came free, Jessie unbuttoned his fly with rapid fingers. The half-breed let her work unhindered, his breath coming in labored gasps as her hand reached inside.

His tumescent length filled her grasp. Jessie let out a breathy cry of delight as she discovered its size. She wrapped her fingers around his manhood and pumped it gently, feeling it stiffen even more in her hand.

Campbell gritted his teeth, hissing into Jessie's ear, "Woman, you are going to kill me, I think. But it is a good night to die."

38

"Hush, James," she said. "I'm going to do no such thing. You might kill me with this thing, though." She flicked her thumb over the knoblike tip of his organ, feeling a drop of moisture there. Her mind reeled as she imagined this weapon inside her, and she felt her own wetness between her legs.

The half-breed pushed his hands down the length of her naked back and cupped her buttocks. Then he reached around to the front of her jeans and fumbled with the buttons there. His large fingers had little success, distracted as he was by her manipulations. Jessie helped him, opening her pants and pulling them off, then stripping her undergarment. She sat there beside him, nude, and tugged at his pants, removing them, along with his boots.

When both of them were naked, the night breezes washing over them, she lay down again with Campbell, her soft hands exploring the length of his taut body. The man, unable to resist the opportunity, slid his own hand between her legs, reaching for the soft patch of hair there. His manhood rested stiffly against her leg as, with one finger, he probed for her wet nether lips; finding the delightful secret chamber that glistened with her moist desire, he slowly inserted his finger.

Jessie gulped air and closed her eyes tightly. Her nails dug into his broad shoulders as she felt him penetrate her with the daring finger. The passage was snug and slick, and he pushed in the entire length of the finger, working it round and round slowly, to prepare her for what was to come.

Then, as he aroused her in this way, his thumb found the sensitive button above the sweet channel and gently rubbed it, causing Jessie to start as a bolt of pleasure shot up her spine.

"James . . . James!" she cooed. She clutched him tighter. This could not be true—loving this big man beneath the open sky, her arms wrapped around his strong torso. She felt his finger move faster, in and out of her, forcing her to the brink.

Suddenly the wave crashed over her and she could not control it. As his thumb touched her, it was like a cannon exploding inside her. She wanted to cry out but dared not. No, this moment was hers, with James alone, and all was darkness, then bright, bright light, as bright as the sun and just as warm. She begged him to stop. "Please, please," she whispered urgently. "Don't..."

Campbell withdrew his hand and pulled her to him, crushing Jessie's breasts against his naked chest, his insistent sword unsheathed and standing between them. He kissed her face and neck, lingering there, brushing his lips against her skin.

She held his steel-hard erection and stroked it, still amazed at its length; she wondered if she would be able to take it all in. The blood-engorged weapon was hot and pulsing with urgency as her fingers slipped up and down upon it.

"I've got to have you, Jessie," the half-breed said in an unsteady voice. And with that he hauled himself up and over her. He lowered his lips to hers. Jessie opened her legs as he lay atop her, easing his weight down so as not to hurt her.

Then she guided the stiff, throbbing sword to the sweet, hotly inviting channel, flicking its tip against the wet lips there. Finally, Jessie helped him enter her, gasping as a dart of stretching pain turned into a deep thrust of pleasure. Suddenly he was inside her to the hilt—and Jessie felt as if she had been impaled to her very core by this strong, silent warrior.

James Campbell lifted himself onto his elbows, his hands holding Jessie's silky smooth shoulders. Jessie raised her legs and locked them around his back, giving him freedom to move. Like an untamed stallion, the man gave her what she wanted. His strokes were long and quick and she lifted her hips to meet him, matching his rhythm, urging him on.

Jessie's mind raced wildly as she made love to him. She thought of her own loneliness, the oftentimes desperate nature of her life on the vengeance trail, the difficult demands of the Starbuck business empire, the many nights she spent without the comfort and excitement of a good man in her bed. She had had other men, but it took a special kind of man to cause her to abandon her troubles, however briefly, in his arms.

James Two Wolves Campbell was, she knew, such a man. In him she saw those intangible qualities of strength and sensitivity and compassion. And yet—she had known him for such a short time. Could it be that she was so in need of love that she had grasped at the first handsome male to come along? No, she assured herself, it was much more than that. This man had awakened in her something that very few men ever did: the undeniable need for love, the desire to share her entire being with another.

Opening her eyes, she saw his dark face above her. A current of pleasure flashed through her body and she felt herself bucking urgently, meeting his thrusts, savoring the near-agony of his animal-like penetration. Yes, she belonged in his arms tonight! What a sharp-edged knife it was that cut into her soul at such a moment...and there was no stopping it, not now...Jessie felt it rising within her, like a bubbling hot spring, ready to gush upward toward the heavens.

Campbell clenched his teeth as he rode her, plunging again and again into her. Then he withdrew from her almost completely and paused for a mere second, gathering his strength before thrusting in again, more deeply than before. His lungs heaved raggedly. Curses and prayers mingled at the edge of his tongue, but he said nothing—for there was nothing to say that would not destroy this supremely beautiful moment.

"James, please love me, never stop..." cried Jessie, as if reading his thoughts.

She writhed beneath him, taking every inch he had to give, wanting more, unable any longer to control her overwhelming desire. It was so sweet, so wild, and if he stopped she knew she would die.

Her fingernails dug into his back as James Campbell bulled her, his strength concentrated wholly on the act of love. Perspiration beaded on his forehead; his arms trembled.

"Woman, I want to . . . make you feel it," he managed to growl, his own voice sounding strange to him.

"Yes, yes," Jessie moaned, bringing her hands to Campbell's neck and pulling his face down to hers. She could not get enough of kissing him, and as he continued to fill her, she tasted his warm lips once again. She smelled the saltiness of his sweat and the burn of the desert wind on his face and tasted his insistent tongue. Even as she thought she wanted more, she felt the impending climax.

He, too, was near the edge. Now he increased his pace, gripping Jessie as he rode harder, giving her all he had. They moved together, she matching his strokes, anticipating his orgasm.

Jessie lifted her legs into the air as her climax washed over her, sending shudders of shocking intensity from one end of her body to the other and back again. "Oh Lord Jesus!" she cried, trying to hold her voice down out here in wide-open country. "James, come with me—oh!" Like a tree halved by lightning, she felt split down the middle. It left her quivering, shaken.

Campbell himself could hold out no longer. With a desperate final thrust into her velvety sheath, he stifled a howl. Then he came, shooting his life essence into her. His manhood remained stiff even as he released every loving drop inside Jessie. He moaned, his eyes clamped shut, his arms hugging her shapely body tightly. And gradually his strokes became slower, until finally he ceased.

"Stay inside me," Jessie told him. A second, less shattering orgasm overcame her, then a pleasantly mellow afterglow. She kept her arms wrapped securely around him

42

so that he could not move away. He lowered himself on top of her and lay with her, breathing heavily, exhausted.

He said, "I hope there are no more Apaches nearby."

"If I have to die tonight, I really wouldn't mind that much."

"We're talking about killing and dying again," Campbell reminded her.

"Then we better hush up." She brushed his hair away from his eyes. "We've made enough noise already on that subject."

*   *   *

When the three rode out early in the morning, after Campbell had stood his turn at watch, Jessie rode at Ki's side. She wondered if he knew that she and the half-breed had made love in the night. Rarely did anything escape Ki's penetrating intelligence, and even if he had not heard them, he would pick up on other clues.

Jessie and Ki's relationship was a complex one, based on mutual dedication to their continuing mission and to the memory of Alex Starbuck, Jessie's father by blood and Ki's chosen *daimyo*—the lord that a samurai served with his entire body and soul. When Alex had been killed, Ki's unswerving devotion went to his daughter, and they vowed together to continue Alex's war against the powerful foreign forces that threatened to destroy their country—Jessie's by birth and Ki's by choice. Such an alliance demanded clarity of mind and heart, a cutting edge of purpose that was like a fine steel blade. It could not include sex, or the sort of love where two people become so bound to each other that their devotion blinds and deafens them to anything but that devotion. If such a thing were to happen to them, it was certain that they would not be allowed a long time to enjoy their blissful state. . . .

The desert sun rose quickly and savagely over the rocks

43

and dunes of gypsum. They had wisely gotten an early start. As Jessie sided him, Ki shielded his eyes and gazed over the final, tough expanse of country through which they had to travel to reach their destination.

"We'll reach Las Cruces by sundown," he said.

Jessie said, "Good. Another night out on the trail would just about do me in."

Ki gave her a sidelong glance, his Oriental eyes dancing darkly. "Sleeping on the cold, hard ground doesn't agree with you?"

"Maybe I'm getting softer," she replied, before she realized the innuendo in his question. She met his gaze frankly. "I thought you had given up caring about where and how I sleep."

A rare smile passed over Ki's placidly composed face. "I care about everything you do, Jessie. You know that. And I care about who you do it with."

"I'm a grown woman now. I can handle myself, Ki," she blazed back with unintentional harshness, immediately regretting her tone.

"You think perhaps I care too much?" Ki inquired, a note of hurt in his voice.

"I like you when you're jealous," Jessie joked. "I didn't mean to bark at you, Ki. I'm sorry," she added. "I couldn't ever hope to have a better friend than you."

Ki loosened his grip on the reins, his horse whickering gratefully. "I must admit to some jealousy toward almost any man you meet," he admitted.

"James is a very good man," said Jessie.

"He is a good fighting man, I agree. And I think he is a smart man as well." The twinkle had returned to Ki's eyes.

Jessie laughed softly. "You two will get along fine."

Campbell rode ahead of them about a half-mile, scouting the trail. Knowing he was out of earshot, Jessie confided in Ki.

"He told me last night that he was riding to Las Cruces to kill a man. Lowell Henry."

Ki's stoic features betrayed no surprise. As his mount loped ahead, he was silent for a long moment. "Did you tell him of our business with the man called Henry?" he asked.

"No," said Jessie. "For some reason I thought it better not to say anything. I did try to talk him out of his crazy idea. But he wouldn't listen to me. His mind is made up."

"Why does he wish to kill this man?"

Jessie told him about James Campbell's mother and other members of the tribe—how they had died of disease-infested meat that Lowell Henry had diverted to the reservation on which they had been confined. A man like that, who could enrich himself at the cost of scores of Indian lives, was not a difficult man to hate.

The desert sun clouded over for a few seconds as she spoke. "It makes me wonder whether we should sell any cattle to him."

"If what Campbell says is true," Ki amended.

"I think he's telling the truth, Ki. Why would he lie to me about it? I just think he's wrong in trying to take the law into his own hands. But he doesn't trust the law—white man's law, he calls it—to get justice."

"I can understand his reasons," Ki said, remembering all the corrupt law officers and judges and lawyers he had encountered in his travels.

Jessie looked out over the vast dry bowl of the desert. Scrub brush and low-slung cactus were the only signs of life. Rocky and dust-covered, the landscape stretched out to reach the distant mountains and cover the earth in desolate bleakness. Uncertainty gripped her as she thought about what lay ahead for her. Knowing what she did about Lowell Henry, she was tempted to take Campbell's allegations to the law herself. Where Indians were concerned, however, she knew the charges would not receive serious attention.

Such dangerous games were played all the time with the lives of reservation-bound tribes. It galled her. White man's "justice."

"We've got to look out for him when we get to Las Cruces," she said to Ki.

"And for ourselves," he reminded her. "A man like this Henry is sure to be wealthy and powerful enough to know about James Campbell, and to know we rode into town with him."

"I should have tried to find out more about him before agreeing to come and talk business. But we do need another market for our cattle." *What would my father have done in a situation like this?* she wondered. Always, her father was a touchstone by which she judged her own actions.

"Your father would have faced Henry head-on, confronted him with the truth, and let him defend himself, if possible," said Ki, as if reading her mind.

Jessie was accustomed to Ki's strange ability to know what she was thinking. Often their thoughts blended together, allowing them to communicate almost without speaking. She said, "I know. That got him in trouble a lot of times, too."

The memory of the man who had raised her almost singlehandedly overcame her, and she closed her eyes to the sunblasted trail. His strong face appeared before her, his constant words of encouragement and advice rang in her ears. What a good man he had been! How angry she still became when she thought of the cowards who had arranged his death, the paid assassins who had done the deed.

Alex Starbuck had been a shrewd businessman—the shrewdest. A pioneer of international trade with the Orient, a successful cattleman, a builder and landowner, Starbuck had left behind a powerful legacy—and powerful enemies who remained bent on destroying the fruits of his hard labors. What would her father do, faced with her present dilemma? He would have aided James Two Wolves Camp-

46

bell in his pursuit of justice, without allowing the half-breed to hurt himself in the process. As for Lowell Henry—Ki was right, she must deal with him honestly but warily. She would let Henry indict himself by his own words and actions.

"Ki, when we get to Las Cruces tonight, I want you to find out what you can about Henry. You're very good at that kind of thing," she said.

"I should have joined the society of the *ninja* and learned how to make myself invisible. Then I would be an even better spy—and encounter much less trouble along the way."

"If you couldn't handle yourself in tough situations, I wouldn't ask you to do this," said Jessie, thinking how invaluable Ki truly was. And she knew that if the time ever came when she had to lay down her own life in exchange for his, she would do it without hesitation.

The riders stopped once in the afternoon to water their horses, then continued on through the desert as the relentless sun beat down upon them. The miles were dry and hard—and long. When Campbell, riding point, sighted the city, Jessie felt immensely relieved. The trip had worn her down; she would need a good night's rest before meeting Lowell Henry in the morning.

In the last hour of their ride, as they pointed their horses into the sun that was about to disappear behind the looming mountains, Campbell stayed closer to Jessie and Ki. At one point he halted the party. He pointed to a series of hoofmarks apart from the trail. "Apache sign," he said. "They were here not more than a day ago."

Jessie said, "There are sure a lot of Apaches in the neighborhood."

"More than I thought," muttered Campbell. "The renegade parties must be growing. But they are riding very close to the city. They usually stay far away."

Less than a quarter of a mile farther down the trail, Campbell spotted wagonwheel ruts—also fresh. He dismounted to inspect the area where the wheel marks stopped. Ki joined Campbell, the two men hunkering together over the ground.

"Look there," Ki said, pointing to an area around the wagon. More pony prints. "The same Apache sign?"

"Yes," said Campbell. "Looks to me like a powwow. Ten or twelve Apaches and a wagon. A white man's wagon. Not many Indians drive wagons."

"That's why they came in so close to town," remarked Ki.

"I don't like the looks of this," Jessie added. "Renegades talking with a white man. Can't be up to any good."

"They were probably trading for whiskey or guns," Campbell said.

The two men remounted and the party rode on, following the wheel ruts. The wagon had driven straight to Las Cruces. On the outskirts of the city, Campbell parted company with Jessie and Ki.

"It would be best if we weren't seen riding in together," he said. "I will find some place to stay—by myself."

"James, I want you to be careful. Where will you be?" Jessie asked.

"The one place in town that will rent me a room, the Posada Dos Cuervos, near the railroad yard. I have stayed there before, and I know the man who owns it. He is trustworthy."

Jessie wasn't convinced that Campbell would be safe anywhere in Las Cruces. She said, "Ki and I will find a hotel nearer the center of town. I'll get word to you, telling you where we are. I'd like to see you tomorrow."

Campbell touched her arm. "I will wait for your message." He then reined around and rode off into the darkness toward Las Cruces.

Ki said, "Come, Jessie, we are almost there."

Chapter 4

Exhausted from the journey, Jessie had supper sent to her room after she had bathed. Ki joined her for the meal and saw that she was safely tucked into bed later. Then he left the hotel for the streets of Las Cruces.

The city lay on a plain at the foot of the San Andres Mountains, on the east bank of the Rio Grande. A bustling center of commerce, it was situated directly north of El Paso, Texas, and to the north, along the river, were Albuquerque and Santa Fe, two hundred and two hundred fifty miles away respectively. Las Cruces had never achieved the importance of those other cities, and it never would; nonetheless, it looked lively enough to Ki as he made his way through the center of town. Hotels and saloons lined the main street, along with a bank and an adobe courthouse left over from the days of the Mexican administration.

Ki turned onto one of the narrower streets and followed it until he came to a brightly lit saloon from which music and laughter rang raucously. He was looking for a place where he could glean information without being noticed, and this seemed to be it.

Inside he saw a long bar to the left side of a big room, with patrons two deep there. Some two dozen tables took up most of the rest of the available space, and these were nearly full. In one corner stood a piano with a man banging away upon it, accompanied by a fellow with a guitar who was trying to sing above the noise—with little success. Looking at the faces of the men here, Ki could see that they were a mixed group of Anglos and Mexicans, working men come to lighten their pockets on cheap whiskey and warm beer. And there were several fancy-dressed girls, serving drinks and joking with the men.

Despite his unusual appearance, Ki slipped practically unnoticed to one end of the bar, sidling in among the crowd to order a beer. The bartender, a skinny man in an immaculate apron, his hair greased back, charged Ki ten cents for a beer, but Ki didn't argue about it. He didn't want trouble on his first night in town, though he knew he was being cheated. He took his beer, sipping it lightly—he did not want to impair his senses, only have a drink in hand so as to fit into the scene—and surveyed the saloon.

He saw a black man playing cards with some Mexicans in one corner of the barroom, a few professional-looking gamblers, some obvious drunks cadging drinks from friends. All in all, it did not add up to anything unusual or particularly significant. He took another sip of his beer and moved out from the bar.

A large man in sweat-stained clothes and a floppy hat stepped in front of him, almost causing Ki to collide with him. The man turned and glared at Ki, but, surprised by his looks and clothing, did not know at first what to say. Ki excused himself and moved on, sensing the man behind him alerting friends to the appearance of the stranger in their midst. Ki felt their eyes on his back and kept walking.

Wherever he went in his travels with Jessie, it seemed that people reacted to him oddly. His manner of dress was unusual—a many-pocketed, well-worn black leather vest over a blousy, collarless white cotton shirt, and on his feet a pair of black, rope-soled cotton slippers. The only commonplace item of clothing he wore was a pair of dusty, faded denim trousers, a concession to the practicalities of life in the unsettled West. Also, his yellow-hued complexion, long straight black hair, and almond-shaped dark eyes tended to attract notice, not always of a pleasant sort; he was commonly mistaken for an Indian, a Mexican, or a Chinese. And the fact that he never carried a gun sometimes sparked trouble from those who thought they could take advantage of him. Ki, though, mistrusted the heavy, unwieldy weapons these men wore, preferring the more subtle and lighter weapons of his own country, which he was trained to use. Now he mentally rechecked his weapons, the *tanto* blade in his waistband and the *shuriken* throwing stars in his vest pockets. If the need arose, Ki could make a weapon out of almost any materials at hand, so he was never completely without the ability to defend himself from unexpected attack.

So he put the unfriendly glares out of his mind and moved on toward the far end of the bar. There he found an opening and put his glass down on the gleaming surface of the bar. The man to Ki's right drained his drink and called to the barkeep for another.

Dressed in a gaudy blue and yellow plaid suit, with a big blue tie that overflowed his chest, the man was in his early thirties. He also wore a derby tilted back on his head, which allowed a shock of brown hair to fall over his forehead. He was obviously drunk—but seemingly enjoying every minute of it. He eyed Ki as the bartender poured his drink.

51

Finally, with that drink in hand, he said, "Hello there. Haven't seen you in here before."

Ki nodded in acknowledgment. "Perhaps because I have never been here before."

The man laughed, exposing a set of big yellow teeth. "I suppose. Not many of—er, your kind hereabouts. You Chinese or something?"

Ki realized that the young man was simply inquiring, not trying to stir up trouble. The drink had loosened his tongue. Ki said, "My mother was Japanese, my father American."

"Figured it was something like that. What brings you here?" He took a quick gulp of his drink, then said, "I forgot to introduce myself. I'm Horace Dunlop." He extended a pale hand.

Ki shook the man's hand. "My name is Ki."

Dunlop squinted quizzically. "That all? Just Ki? Well, I suppose it's better to have a simple handle. Easier for the girls to remember, eh?" He winked—with some difficulty.

"Yes, it is," Ki agreed, not knowing quite what to make of this flamboyant character. He sipped carefully on his beer, waiting for Dunlop to say what was on his mind.

"Now, in my business it's important to remember names—and for my name to be remembered too. I represent a Kansas City concern. Perhaps you've heard of us—the Preferred Products Company, Incorporated." Dunlop fumbled in his jacket and produced an embossed business card bearing his name and the name and address of his company. "There, you see, that's me. I travel all over the West, presenting my company's products to merchants. I'm an assistant sales manager. One day I plan to be *the* sales manager." He took another drink to bolster his argument in his own mind. "Yes sir, I'm headed for big things. I'm much appreciated in the home office, I can assure you. They have plans for me."

"I congratulate you," said Ki. He had found a live one—a man who loved to talk. Perhaps this fellow knew something of Lowell Henry. He asked Dunlop how long he had been in town.

"Just a week. I'll be here for another week, at least. Still have several calls to make."

Ki guided the conversation to the topic of business conditions in Las Cruces, and those with whom Dunlop did business. Dunlop reeled off some names that meant nothing to Ki, who then asked him point blank, "Do you know Mr. Lowell Henry?"

"Know him? No. Know *of* him, yes. He's the biggest"—Dunlop looked around the saloon to be sure no one was listening—"the biggest son of a bitch in town—rich, shrewd, ruthless—a good man to do business with if you have something he wants. Wouldn't want to get in his way, though, not from what I've heard about him."

"What have you heard about him?"

"Well, he's too smart to get caught at it, but the rumor is that he gets his way by whatever means necessary—if you catch my meaning." Dunlop finished off his drink and signaled to the barman to fetch another. "A few bashed-in heads, a few widows, some bankruptcies—the usual thing. Mr. Lowell Henry seems to get his way in this town, that's for sure."

Not surprising, thought Ki, but nothing particularly solid. He wanted to know specifically what sort of businesses Henry was involved in besides cattle—and what sort of political connections the man had. Ki suspected that Henry was very well connected.

Dunlop was not of much further help, though. He said, "I stay away from men like Henry. I can't help him, and he can't help me." The drummer hiccoughed loudly. " 'Scuse me, Mr. Ki."

Behind him, Ki heard a girl's laughter, then her voice: "You've had too much to drink, Señor Dunlop."

Dunlop said, "I've lost count, Señorita, begging your pardon."

Ki turned to face a beautiful bar girl. Her raven-black

hair was piled high atop her head, leaving her olive-complexioned face to shine prettily. Dark brown eyes returned his direct gaze. And her delightful shape was barely concealed in the short skirt she wore. All in all, she was a fine-looking young woman—not yet twenty, Ki guessed.

"Good evening, Señor," she said to Ki.

Dunlop, a bit flustered by her appearance, regained his composure long enough to introduce her. "Mr. Ki, this is Señorita Rita—that kind of rhymes, you see. Rita, this is Mr. Ki, from—" He looked blankly at Ki. "You never told me where you're from."

"Texas," Ki said simply, bowing to the girl.

She smiled brightly and said, "My pleasure, Señor Ki. I'm just looking after Señor Dunlop. Sometimes he needs help getting home."

"Now when have I ever—" Dunlop drew himself up to his full height, no more than five and a half feet, and thrust his chin out indignantly. "I challenge you to prove that."

"You don't remember the night before last, then?" the girl asked him, her hands on her rounded hips. Her dark eyes flashed playfully.

"Let me see . . ." Dunlop removed his derby and scratched his head. "Now that you remind me, I seem to remember I had a wee bit too much in the libation department—but I woke up in my own bed, seems to me." With that, he finished off half of his drink.

Ki couldn't take his eyes off the girl, Rita, as she challenged Dunlop. There was a real spark of life in her—a tone of authority and independence—that contradicted the faint glimmer of sadness in her brown eyes. There were many saloon girls who didn't want to be saloon girls, and she looked to be one of those—yet she retained a remarkable measure of pride and self-esteem—and fresh good looks.

He liked her and felt an insistent stirring within himself. What was it about her, as she stood there amid the rowdy, liquid, smoky atmosphere of the saloon, that betrayed her

54

essential vulnerability? And he sensed in her unwavering gaze that somehow she was interested in him. But if there was something between the girl and Dunlop, Ki would not think of interfering.

Just then a noise caused Ki to turn back to where Dunlop was standing—except that the drummer was no longer standing there. He had collapsed in a heap in front of the bar. He lay there with a wide smile plastered on his face, his derby on the floor beside him. Ki bent to help him up as the other men at the bar turned away, laughing. Rita took one of Dunlop's arms and Ki took the other, and they hauled him to his feet. He stood there, wavering madly, his eyes half closed. He hiccoughed again, his head jerking back comically. Rita retrieved his hat and planted it on his head firmly.

"Where is he staying?" Ki asked.

"Just two blocks from here," the girl said. "I can manage."

"I will carry him," said Ki, hoisting the drummer into his arms.

"I—I'd like to go with you," she said. "I'll show you to his hotel."

Ki relented, wondering why she was so insistent. They made their way through the packed saloon and out into the dark, cool street. It was a simple matter of getting Dunlop's key from the weary hotel clerk and depositing the man on his bed, then locking the door behind them as they left. Ki thanked the girl and offered to escort her back to the bar.

She said, "I'd rather not go back, Señor." Her eyes dropped, and Ki thought she was about to cry. "But I don't have anyplace else to go, so perhaps I'd better..."

As they left the hotel, Ki said, "What is wrong, Rita?" She did not answer. "Why do you work there if that is not what you want to do?" he asked.

The girl stopped in the middle of the street. "I need the work, Señor Ki. I am alone here. There is nothing else for a girl like me—nowhere else. But I want you to understand . . . oh, it is no use!" The tears came, finally. "No use at all!"

Putting a hand on her shoulder, Ki said, "Where do you live?"

"Over on the north end of town, near the railroad station. I have a room there among my people—other Mexicans. It is my home, until I can find a better place."

"Let me take you there," offered Ki. "I do not want you to go back to the saloon tonight."

She was torn for a moment. As much as she hated her job as a fancy girl, how else could she make a living? If she thought she was meant for better things, how in the world would she ever get to the place where she could prove it? Ki seemed to know that these questions were running through her mind. He allowed her to make up her own mind. She decided to let him walk her home.

He tried to get her to talk about herself, but she would not. Together they made their way through the back streets of Las Cruces, where the poorer people lived—most of them Mexican or part Indian—in small houses and even shacks. Some had a few domestic animals, such as pigs or chickens, in pens near their homes. Dogs barked loudly as Ki and Rita passed, and he heard babies crying all along the way to the girl's place.

They reached the building where she lived, a two-story boarding house with no lights on to indicate that anyone was home. She assured him that the landlady was there, and at least two other tenants. Signaling to him to be quiet, she led him up the back stairway to the second floor, then inside. The hallway was narrow and pitch black. The girl found her way to her room and let herself in, asking Ki to come in too.

She closed the door and went to light a lamp, keeping the flame low. In the eerie glow of the lamp, Ki could see the room—small, cramped, but neatly arranged. She did not possess many clothes, or anything else but a small plaster statue of the Virgin Mary and a cracked, framed mirror, both of which stood on a small table near the bed.

Rita invited Ki to sit on the bed, which he did, feeling the lumpy straw mattress. She poured some water from a pitcher into a bowl and washed her face and hands, drying herself afterward on a ragged towel. Then she sat beside him on the bed.

"Thank you," she said, "for understanding. I do not know what to do, Señor Ki. I cannot return to my family—they are in Juarez—but I hate my job at that place. The men, they are sometimes so cruel to me, they use me and humiliate me. Every night I pray to the Blessed Virgin and ask her to help me. But nothing happens. I feel like a prisoner here sometimes. There are some nice men, like Señor Dunlop, but most of them are—"

She could not finish the sentence. Ki said, "Why did you leave your family?"

"They are very poor. I was one of twelve children. They do not even miss me, I am certain. My older brother and sister also left when they came of age. I was always hungry. I did not want to be hungry ever again."

Ki put his arm around her. She was small, afraid. He felt sad for her, and at the same time, here alone in her room, he felt the attraction any man feels for a young, pretty woman. Yet he told himself that he would not take advantage of her, that the *bushido* code would not allow such behavior.

Rita had a different idea, though. "Señor Ki," she whispered. She placed a soft kiss on his cheek. "Stay with me tonight. Please."

"You are a beautiful girl," he said. "I do not wish to force myself on you."

"You are not forcing yourself," Rita insisted. "I asked you." She paused, considering her words carefully. "Ki, I have had men—many men—but few of them had any love

57

or respect for me. I had no love for any of them, even the kindest ones. Most of them smelled bad and used me in disgusting ways. I have learned a lot from these men—things no girl should ever know. And yet...I do not feel dirty with you. I need your love, Ki, to make me feel clean through and through. Do this for me, I beg you."

In the soft golden glow of the lamp, her upturned face took on an added mysterious quality. Her tears had dried, and now determination framed her delicate features. She knew what she wanted from this man, and she was bound to get it.

She kissed him again, and this time Ki turned to meet her lips with his own. Almost violently their mouths came together. The girl responded by throwing her arms around him, wanting this man to take total control of her—mind and body. Ki was the most fascinating man she had ever met; his lithe body, his intelligence, his exotic handsomeness were unlike anything she had encountered in the men who came to the saloon looking for pleasure.

The next moment they were undressing each other. Rita marveled at Ki's smooth muscles, his golden skin, his clean, manly scent. She sought to touch every inch of him, her hands roaming over the lean lines of his shoulders, chest, torso, back, until finally she touched the erect organ that sprang from the thick black thatch between his strong legs.

Ki found her body beautiful: her brown-tipped breasts perfectly formed; her narrow, tapered waist; the sensuous flare of her curving hips; her lovingly sculptured legs, which hung now over the side of the bed. He drank her in, stunned by the suddenness of their intimacy, but too excited to wonder very much why he was in her room this night. An inner urgency possessed him, for it had been a long time since he had been with a woman.

Together they lay back on the bed, each exploring the secrets of the other's body. Rita then made the first move, impelled by a deep, womanly craving that had to be fulfilled by this man and no other. She brought her warm, full lips to his, and they kissed hungrily. Ki sent his tongue between her lips, writhing into her mouth. She accepted it, and their tongues entwined wetly. They lingered deliciously, deliberately, neither wanting this moment to end.

When they pulled apart, the girl asked him, "Where did you learn to kiss like that?"

Ki smiled. "In my country I learned the way of the samurai warrior. There is an art to conquest on the battlefield and in the bed of love. I had good teachers in both arts."

"Where do you come from, Ki?"

"From a land far away from here, across the great sea called the Pacific. I came here many years ago with a man, an American. He was like a father to me in many ways, and I had been without father or mother for a long time. In gratitude I dedicated my life to serving him. He is now dead and I serve his only child. That is my life, Señorita," he concluded with a slow smile.

She placed her hand on his bare chest. "You are a strange man, but I like you very much." Her hand fell to his manhood, and she squeezed it lovingly and stroked it.

He breathed into her ear, his tongue darting there, as her hand moved. All faraway thoughts were driven from his brain. He kissed her ear and neck, biting gently as he found her tender, curving shoulder. She moaned and released his rigid member.

"Oh, Ki," she breathed. "Make love to me. I want you so much."

Ki moved above her, his lips caressing her flesh. He burned a trail down her neck, over her chest, to the proud twin mounds of her breasts. Now, with his wet tongue, he traced mystical patterns there before taking an erect brown nipple into his mouth. Rita shuddered and then stiffened slightly, but she relaxed then and let him fondle and suck her there. His teeth moved over a dark, budding nipple and he heard her moan with surprise and pleasure. She was

59

letting him take control now, he knew.

With his free hand, Ki reached down to explore the silky smoothness of her inner thigh. Her skin was marvelous to the touch, as warm as a sandy seaside beach, as smooth as a piece of the finest silk from his homeland. His fingertips stroked her there and touched gently at the love nest at the juncture of her dark thighs. Then, with two fingers, he probed lightly until he found what he was searching for: the small mound of flesh that unlocked the secret treasure of every woman. Rita shuddered at his touch. Carefully, slowly, lovingly, he rubbed, sliding his finger round and round, feeling her wetness increase. Ki brought her to the edge of the abyss with sure, even stimulation before he pulled away.

The girl stifled a cry and looked down at him. Ki slid his arms underneath her and lifted her up farther on the bed, until her head rested high on her pillow and her navel lay beneath his face. He gave a playful flick of his tongue to her navel, and Rita laughed in surprise.

"Señor Ki!" she exclaimed.

Ki did not answer her; he lowered his head, spreading her velvety legs at the same time. When she realized what he was doing, Rita gasped, but she did nothing to stop him. She was completely in his hands.

Ki buried his face in her steaming sex, and teased and tortured her with his expert tongue. Rita squirmed and bucked as he licked her, swirling in and out of her flesh, pressing the tender nub, which responded by stiffening under his ministrations.

She could not help crying out, "Yes, Ki! That feels good. Oh, please—so nice, so good!" Her words were followed by muffled, guttural sounds as she succumbed to a quivering, shattering climax.

Ki could feel her body registering the orgasm, and he looked up to see her beautiful face raised to heaven, her mouth open as if in prayer. He kissed her sex once again and raised himself atop her. She threw her arms around his neck and yanked him down to kiss him.

Their lips burned together hotly as her fingers groped once again for the tumescent length of his love-spear. Then she found it and guided it into her. She was ready for him, and Ki slid in easily.

Rita gasped, "Oh, you're wonderful. Ki. There is so much of you. I want it all."

Ki, unable to speak for the tension building within his groin, pumped his manhood far into her deep chamber. The girl opened her legs for him, taking every inch willingly. Her little cries sounded through the dark room.

The samurai struggled with some difficulty to control his rhythm. He wanted to bring Rita along with him before he came. She moved to meet his thrusts, her hips begging him to do it harder.

Their bodies melded together, Ki pumping strongly, the girl answering his every stroke with sighing sounds that came from the very core of her being. Never had she experienced a lover like this strange, lithe man from a land across the sea. He brought her alive, every bit of her, and she abandoned herself to him without question.

"Yes, my love . . . please . . . make me feel you . . . I want all of you."

Her words barely penetrated the hot fog that enshrouded his brain. His own deep need possessed him now. He struggled to discipline his lovemaking, and with every stroke he knew Rita, too, was building toward the moment of final release.

Ki thrust faster, lifting the girl from the bed. Suddenly it gripped them both—a shattering eruption. She felt him explode inside her, giving her everything he had, as an overpowering shudder bolted from her head to her toes. They bucked against each other, flesh meeting searing flesh.

Within a few moments it was over, and they lay together quietly. Ki stroked her hair and the girl hugged him tightly to her. Neither wanted to let go—not just yet. The blue-gold flame sputtered in the lamp beside the bed and caused their shadows to dance on the opposite wall. Even the lumpy mattress beneath them felt as luxurious as the soft grass of a hidden meadow—as if they had been transported to another place altogether.

"You are a strong man, Ki," she teased him. "Too strong for a little girl like me."

"A little girl? You are a woman," he answered. "You are every bit a woman."

"Only you can make me feel that way," said Rita. "I never knew it could be like this. I never thought . . ."

"That is only because you have not yet met the right man. When you do, you will find that it can often be like this."

"I—I wish you were that man, Ki," she murmured softly, still clutching him, not wanting him to leave her. "I don't think there is anyone else like you."

Ki's heart went out to this girl. She was smart, she was loving, and she had had too many things go wrong for her. Why couldn't she find a good man? Yet he knew that he was not the man for her; his life was already determined, his karma decided.

He told her, "I will not be here for long—a few days at most. But while I am here, I will do anything I can for you."

Tears spilled from her eyes onto Ki's chest. He cradled her head there as she sobbed. She asked him, "Why must you go away? If you loved me—"

"I told you, I think you are a beautiful girl. But even if I wanted to stay with you here, I could not. My vow to the family I serve takes me to many places. That is the nature of my life, as I said. I cannot change that."

Rita pulled away from him. Almost angrily she said, "Then you do not love me."

"You are a woman. You know whether I do or do not," he said simply.

Ki dressed as the girl lay there, her back turned to him. He slipped on his pants, shirt, and vest, then sat on the bed to put on his rope-soled slippers. He bent to kiss her before he left.

She turned and threw her arms around him. She didn't know what to say—she kissed him instead. Her lips clung longingly to his. "Señor Ki, I am sorry for what I said."

"You need not be sorry, Rita. I understand. And I wish the best for you. Someday you will leave this town far behind. If you work for that day, it will happen."

The girl shook her head sadly. "I do not know if I am that strong. By myself—without a man, without money—I do not know what I can do."

"First, find another job than the one you have at the saloon. You are not respected there. Go where you can earn a wage and look upon yourself with pride."

She nodded. Again she looked away from Ki, to prevent him from seeing her weep. "Goodbye," she said.

"Goodbye, Rita," Ki replied. He closed the door and made his way out through the darkness. It was late now, approaching midnight. There were few people out on the streets.

Ki tried to put aside thoughts of the lonely girl. He hoped he had said the right things to her, that he had not hurt her. Should he not have made love to her, he wondered. No, he had done the right thing; both of them had needed love tonight. She was a good young woman, intelligent enough to realize the truth of the matter.

The samurai asked a passerby the location of the Posada Dos Cuervos. Several blocks west. Ki suddenly decided to look in on James Campbell, figuring that no one would see him at this time of night. And something inside him—a warrior's instinct, perhaps—told him to check up on the half-breed.

The street was narrow and crooked, with no plankwalks joining the many buildings, but only dirt littered with horse droppings and rutted by big-wheeled wagons. This part of the city was redolent of fried meat and tortillas. A squawling child broke the night silence. From the tall mountain to the east, Ki supposed one could look down upon the whole of Las Cruces and see all the houses laid out along these streets, and all the places where people did business, and the big church where some of them worshipped God. But from street level, in the blackness, the smells and sounds guided him instead, as he walked quietly on his way.

Ki reached the *posada* after a few minutes: the inn was a small, dilapidated structure that needed repair badly, yet still somehow stood erect. The front door squeaked loudly on its hinges as Ki pushed it open. An abandoned desk stood near a staircase. A man snored in a wooden chair behind the desk. Ki went up to him and awakened him. Startled, the man spun out a series of oaths in Spanish, then asked Ki what he wanted.

"I want to see the man called James Campbell. I am a friend."

"Señor Campbell has few friends," the innkeeper said in English. "He is not here. I have not seen him for years."

Ki saw that the man was lying to protect Campbell. He must have been Campbell's friend for a long time, and was used to putting people off the half-breed's trail. But Ki assured the innkeeper that he was Campbell's friend, too. "Did he tell you of a woman and a man with whom he rode to Las Cruces?" Ki asked.

"*Sí*. A woman and a man." His eyes narrowed as he looked at Ki more closely. "A man like you, with slanted eyes. *Sí*." He scratched his stubbly chin, mulling the evidence over for another few moments. Then he said, "I am Roberto Flores, owner of this place, such as it is," and he gestured futilely at the state of the inn.

He told Ki that Campbell could be found in Room Four, upstairs. He urged Ki to stand aside from the door as he knocked, for Campbell was prepared to greet unwelcome visitors more than friends at this hour.

Ki thanked him and made his way upstairs as Flores took his place in the chair and promptly nodded off again. Ki had a bad feeling about this place. As loyal as Flores seemed, he did not provide adequate protection for Campbell. He'd talk to Campbell about that. In the murky darkness of the hallway, he found the room.

He raised his hand to knock on the door—standing to one side as the innkeeper had wisely advised—when he felt a sudden, sharp blow to the back of his head. . . .

★

Chapter 5

Through the knifing pain, Ki tried to think. He could not tell whether his eyes were opened or closed, because everything was black. Then he heard the shuffling of feet—more than one man, but he could not tell how many. Then there was a crash. Ki lifted his head and saw the door to Campbell's room splinter and fall open. The man rushed past him into the room.

Ki struggled to his knees and peered inside through the darkness. Clutching the doorframe, he got to his feet. There was a shout. He saw three—no four—silhouetted figures moving in the room. His head felt like a split-open watermelon. Unsteadily he took a step into the room.

An explosion and a blue-orange flame blasted from one corner of the room. One man screamed. In the momentary flash of light, Ki saw James Campbell firing his revolver. One of the intruders took a bullet in the chest and fell to the floor. The two other men jumped Campbell.

Forgetting the pain in his head, Ki leaped into action, collaring one of the attackers and prying him loose from Campbell. He spun the man around with one hand and brought the heel of his other hand up in a strike to the chin. The man's teeth clamped together with a jarring clack and, stunned, the attacker fell back against a wall. Ki followed with a swift sideways kick to the man's midsection, driving the air from his lungs.

Turning to help Campbell, Ki saw that the half-breed was in trouble. The third attacker held Campbell in a bear hug, his arms locked around his victim's arms, the revolver hanging uselessly from Campbell's hand. The gun clattered to the floor as Campbell attempted to break free, but the attacker clamped his arms even harder, making it difficult for Campbell to breathe.

Ki slipped an arm around the front of the attacker's neck, tightening it, giving the man a taste of his own medicine. Campbell saw what was happening and gathered his strength in one driving elbow blow to the attacker's gut, thrusting it into the man with everything he had. The man weakened, but retained his grip on the half-breed.

Ki groped for an *atemi* point on the attacker's neck to put him out once and for all. But the man sensed what Ki was trying to do and suddenly released Campbell and swung around, breaking Ki's lock on his neck. He loosed a wide roundhouse right at Ki's face, but the samurai brought up his left arm in a revolving upper block, fending off the blow.

The second man, whom Ki had put out of commission, was now stirring again. He came to, saw what was happening, and edged his way toward the door. His partner, jumping back to avoid a slicing kick by Ki, turned and saw the second attacker stand and bolt out the door. "Goddammit, come back here!" he bellowed. Now he stood alone, facing Ki and Campbell. It took him only a second to decide to join the other man—and he, too, was out the door in a flash.

Ki went to Campbell, who had retrieved his revolver from the floor. "Are you all right?"

The tall half-breed nodded. "I had a feeling they would come for me tonight. I should have been able to down two of them, but they were too quick."

The two men bent over the dead man, who was lying in a pool of dark blood, a gaping bullet wound in his chest. Campbell searched his pockets and found only a twenty-dollar gold piece. He appropriated the money. "These boys were paid to visit me," he said.

Sensing the urgency of the situation, Ki said, "I think we should pursue the others—make them talk if we can."

"Right," said Campbell, grabbing his holster and buckling it on as he followed Ki out the door.

The two men ran down the front steps and through the lobby, passing the innkeeper, Flores, who shouted, "What the hell is going on up there? Somebody get shot?" But Ki and Campbell couldn't stop to answer him.

Once out on the street, they paused and looked in both directions, uncertain. Then Campbell said, "This way," and took off. Ki followed him closely, matching his long strides.

They ran through the dark, close streets, Campbell turning up one, then down another. An experienced tracker, he relied as much on instinct as on what little sign he could pick up. Within a few minutes, Ki knew they were nearing the attackers; he heard their footsteps ahead, treading along one of the side streets.

Campbell said, "We have to keep quiet, surprise them." He slowed his pace a bit, moving as stealthily as a wolf on the prowl. His Indian training showed.

"Are you planning to use that gun?" Ki asked, worried that any such noise would draw a crowd—the last thing they wanted.

"Not unless I have to. I'd rather break their necks with

my bare hands—after we find out who paid them to come after me."

The half-breed signaled for Ki to flatten himself against a wall, in the deepest shadow of the street. Ki complied, and Campbell moved with him. In this way the two men made their way to a narrow lane, almost an alley, and slipped around the corner. Then they ran to the other end, which opened onto a wider street. And there they saw the two attackers, walking now, nervously watching their backtrail.

With the silent swiftness of eagles swooping down from the sky to capture their prey, Ki and James Campbell shot from their cover toward the two strangers. The two barely had time to realize what was happening as Ki and Campbell fell upon them. All four men went down in a heap in the dust.

Ki then jumped to his feet. His man was the smaller of the two, though he was big enough—just under six feet tall, with wide shoulders and long arms and a mop of curly red hair. His face, twisted in anger and surprise, revealed a previously broken nose and a pair of dark, close-set eyes. He rolled to one side as Ki tried to pin him down with a flat-footed kick to the midsection. He recovered and sprang to his feet, his arms lowered, challenging Ki to come at him.

The samurai circled the man, closing the gap between them as he did so. The redhead swung at him and Ki ducked, feeling the rush of air over his head as the fist barely missed him. Upright once again, Ki blocked another blow with his arm and, with his free hand, shot a palm-heel strike into the man's face. He felt the man's nose flatten beneath his hand, the bone and cartilage shattering and blood spraying in every direction. The redhead howled like a kicked dog and backed away, bringing his hand to his injured face.

Meanwhile, Campbell faced his opponent, a big man with a barrel chest and hairy, muscular arms. This man wore a beard streaked with gray, and a floppy hat that obscured his eyes. He moved deliberately, his giant, hamlike fists raised like those of a prizefighter. The half-breed tried to sting him with a series of quick rights and lefts, but the big man was not flustered, retaining his defensive stance, moving like an angry bear.

Then the big man let loose with a vicious left that connected with the side of Campbell's head, stunning him for a second. The stranger followed with a right to the stomach, bending Campbell over. As Campbell straightened, he brought his own right fist up, smashing into the big man's Adam's apple, causing him to gurgle in pain. The half-breed planted a right, then a left in the man's substantial gut, and felt the heavy muscles there.

The man took the blows without flinching; he flailed out, catching Campbell once again on the side of the head, making his ears ring. Campbell shook his head and danced back for breathing room, then advanced, determined to deal out some punishment. He knew that the big man had stamina and strength, and that he would have to wear him down, as he avoided the killing blows the man was capable of dishing out.

Ten feet away, Ki had a mad bull on his hands. His bloodied face a mask of rage, the redhead came back for more. Ki kept him at bay with a series of front and side kicks, causing him to move off balance. The samurai's arms windmilled as his legs thrust out at the man, and then he resumed the static *te* fighting stance, gathered his breath, and launched a knife-hand blow to the redhead's neck. The hand stunned the man briefly, and he responded by charging Ki, his eyes glittering with hate.

Ki was surprised by the man's sudden move and tried to dodge out of the way of his charge. But the redhead was able to reach Ki, envelop him in his arms, and bring him to the ground. Ki felt the man's bulk fall on top of him, crushing him to the dust. With one lithe arm the samurai tried to push the man's face away. The redhead reached for Ki's neck, wrapping his strong fingers around it and attempting to strangle him. Ki felt his breath being cut off, his windpipe constricted. He pushed now with both hands, to no effect. The bloody face grinned at him, revealing a row of blackened, uneven teeth. It was like a death mask. Desperately, Ki reached for his enemy's neck, but found that his strength was ebbing. He had to do something else.

Finally, as he squirmed beneath the redhead, he freed his right leg and brought it up in a quick, jarring knee thrust to the man's groin. Immediately the hands loosened around his neck—but they didn't let go. Ki tried it again as his opponent tried to maneuver to the side. This time his knee hit the redhead's pubic bone and forced the man to release his neck. Ki pushed him off and rolled through the dust to escape.

Campbell had traded blows with the bearded attacker, to no effect. The man was too strong to be matched. Campbell would have to wear him down—if he could. He glanced over to Ki, saw that his companion was having a struggle of his own. And in that brief lapse in his concentration, Campbell felt a big fist crash into his jaw, loosening a tooth. Blood erupted from his mouth as his head snapped back. Cursing himself for a fool, he backpedaled, avoiding another blow from the bearlike man.

His head was fogged from the repeated beating, and Campbell tried to clear it as he moved away from the man. But the big man kept coming. He lumbered across the dusty street, his eyes locked on the half-breed, a sneer on his bearded face. Campbell let him come, resigned to whatever would happen, hoping he could sneak in one good fist between the man's sturdy defenses.

The four men raised a cloud of dust in the street as they fought, the darkness interrupted only by a faint glow from the distant crescent moon. If there was anyone watching them, it wasn't apparent, for no one emerged from the buildings along the street, no cry of alarm was raised.

The big man bore down on Campbell, who crouched low, his fists raised. Luckily he was able to block a crashing left from the enemy, and then he pummeled the man's midsection with his own left, finally feeling that he was having some effect. The big man halted for a moment, then came on again, propelling his giant fists against Campbell's ineffective blocks. Like the pistons on a steam engine, the bearded man's arms moved relentlessly—but a bit more slowly than they had at first. Campbell sensed this and an idea came to him.

He took several more blows, letting the big man tire himself. Then, using his arms to shield himself, he crouched again. Exploding upward, Campbell pried the enemy's arms apart with his own and brought his head up, smashing it into the man's jaw. Despite the pain it caused, he did it again—then again, this time bucking his skull against the man's outthrust chin. This stood the big man upright and dropped his arms. His hat lay ten feet away in the dirt.

Campbell followed with hard punches to his opponent's now-weakened stomach, driving him back.

Ki had gained an advantage over his dazed rival, who was staggering toward him. He met the redhead with a high-arcing roundhouse kick, catching him in the ear and taking away his balance. He teetered in one direction and then another, but stayed on his feet. His small, piglike eyes stared at Ki, and his face was a pulpy mess, spattered with blood.

Now was the time, Ki knew, to finish him off. Ki darted forward, unleashing a savage, straight-on kick to the enemy's chest. The redhead was driven back. The samurai came on, lunging forward with chopping knife-hand blows to the neck that stunned the man with their violence and precision, rocking his head back. Then Ki reached under and planted a quick, hard fist in the redhead's midsection that pushed the air out of his lungs and doubled him over. Bringing his right knee up, Ki connected again with the man's face, battering it even more, sending the man screaming into the dust.

Ki then turned to James Campbell and the bearded man, to see if he could be of any help.

Campbell was standing his ground, taking punishment

from the big man, but giving as good as he got, slipping punches in around the man's weakening defenses, attacking every part of his body. The half-breed warded off a series of stiff-arm blows, feeling the tide turn in his favor as he peppered his opponent's belly with rights and lefts from close range. The bearded man's heavily muscled flesh quivered under the renewed attack, and Campbell continued to pummel him with all his strength.

Then a roundhouse right to the man's cheekbone was rewarded as the half-breed watched him topple to the ground like a felled redwood. The big man lay there, out cold. Ki turned to the redheaded man, who was stirring again.

Campbell wiped the blood from his mouth and wearily walked over to Ki. Both men caught their breaths as they stood over the redheaded stranger, whose face and shirt were covered with blood.

"Where did you come from?" Campbell asked Ki.

Ki pushed his black hair out of his eyes. "I had a bad feeling," he explained. "So I came."

"Sure you're not part Indian, like me?"

Ki said, "I might as well be." He toed the downed man in the ribs. "This one will talk."

Campbell hunkered down over the man, who spat blood with every breath. "Who are you, mister?" he asked. The redhead blinked at him, his eyes shifting from Campbell to Ki. "I asked you a question," the half-breed growled. He was in no mood for games.

"Bobby Stella," the man croaked. "I—we only wanted to hurt you a little bit. We didn't mean no harm by it. We—"

"Shut up," Campbell ordered. "Who sent you after me?"

Like a caged possum, Stella withered in helpless fear. It hadn't gone according to plan. He said, "I dunno—just got some money. He talked to the man." The redhead gestured at his partner. "He gave Joey and me the money—twenty dollars each—didn't want to tell us who wanted the job done."

"What's your friend's name?" asked Campbell.

"That's Art French. He hurt bad?" Stella raised his head to look over at his friend.

"Bad enough. How do you know him?" The half-breed was not moved by the man's plight. If whoever had paid them ever found out that this boy had talked, that would be the end of him. Campbell took hold of his shirt collar and yanked his head off the ground, then dropped it.

"Ouch! No call to do that, mister," Stella whined.

"Tell me how you know this man French," Campbell demanded.

"Used to work with him," the redhead sputtered. "Done a few . . . jobs together."

"What kind of jobs?"

"Anything that paid—little rustling, roughing a few guys up, that sort of thing, mostly."

"And he never told you who was paying the rent? Speak up, man. French never told you?"

"No—no—he never—" Stella gulped, swallowing blood and saliva, choking on it. His eyes retreated in terror as he looked at the dark-faced half-breed who interrogated him. "I never asked, neither. Figured it best I never knowed."

"You stupid asshole," Campbell spat. "Then there's no reason we should let you live. You intended to kill me. Now it's your turn to die."

"No—wait!" the man cried. "Art told me something. Never said the name. But—"

Movement flickered in the corner of Ki's eye, and he looked over to where Art French lay in the street. The bearded man held a revolver in his hand and was bringing it up, taking aim at Campbell's exposed back.

"Look out—behind you!" Ki called, diving to the dust and taking a *shuriken* throwing star from his vest pocket. As he fell, he released the razorlike disk with a practiced flick of his wrist.

At Ki's shouted warning, Campbell reached for his gun, clearing leather in a split second. He brought the barrel up

75

as he swung to face French. Cocking and leveling it in one smooth motion, the half-breed squeezed the trigger. The gun flamed in the night, the report echoing off the surrounding structures, and a bullet pierced the big man's neck—causing him to discharge his weapon into the dirt.

As French fell back, dead, Campbell saw a gleaming object embedded between the man's eyes. A ribbon of blood running down French's face mingled with the river flowing from his neck.

"What the hell is that?" Campbell asked Ki as both men stood.

Ki walked over to the dead Art French, planted a foot on his face, and used it for leverage as he pried the *shuriken* from the man's forehead. Then Ki wiped the star-shaped blade clean on the man's shirt and showed it to Campbell, who was impressed.

"Never saw one of those before," he told the samurai. "You're just full of tricks, aren't you?" He smiled slightly in the dim light. "Trickier than an Indian," he added, and went on, "That's twice tonight you've saved my life. Not a thing a man forgets."

"Is he dead? Did you kill him? You sonsabitches, you killed Art!" wailed Stella.

Campbell swung his big revolver around and planted the business end of the barrel at Stella's head. "Tell me what you know, you gutless dog, or I'll spill what little brains you've got."

"All right, all right! Art—he worked for a man here in town. I don't know who, but I know he—the man—did a lot of business with the Apaches, the ones running wild out in the desert. Traded with them—guns and whiskey. Once Art asked me to go with him, but I didn't. I—I was scared—didn't want to lose my scalp. Jesus, mister, that's all I know. I swear it! Don't kill me—please."

Begging for his life, the man was a pitiful sight.

Ki looked at Campbell. He knew they were both thinking

of the wagon ruts they had seen, riding into town this evening. How the hell did that tie in with the attack on Campbell?

"Take care of your friend," the half-breed told Bobby Stella. "His share of the money ought to buy a decent burial—which is more than he deserves. And you better haul your ass out of this town and don't say anything to anybody. That's more than you deserve, but we'll let you go." Campbell softly replaced the hammer and holstered his revolver.

Tears sprang from the downed man's close-set eyes. "I told you everything I know. I swear it."

Campbell said, "I believe it. And I don't want to see your ugly face ever again."

Ki and Campbell left the man there to nurse his wounds and see to his dead friend.

* * *

Ki took James Campbell back to the hotel, where they awoke Jessie. She was shocked at their condition—bloodied and disheveled from the fight in Campbell's room and out in the street. She got the story from them as she helped clean their cuts, listening intently as they related the details, including what Stella had said.

"The local law is not going to appreciate this," Campbell said. "Two dead bodies in one night. I won't be welcome for very long, once they find out who did it."

"But you were attacked in your room," Jessie pointed out. "You were only defending yourself."

"The word of a half-Indian against the lives of two white men isn't worth much."

"Also Ki's word," Jessie said, but she knew that what he said was true. Campbell would be unwelcome in this city until it could be proved that someone had paid the three men to kill him. But who had done it?

Campbell said, "It's best that I leave town, at least for

77

a while. The longer I'm here, the more dangerous it is for you. Flores and Stella both saw Ki and me together. Even though I trust Flores, they might force him to talk. It doesn't look good for us," he concluded.

"Where will you go?" asked Jessie.

"To the desert. I must strengthen my medicine. The wolf god must be displeased with me, to allow this to happen." Jessie noticed the faintest trace of a smile. She was sitting on her bed in a nightgown, and could feel his eyes on her body. "Except for you two friends, I would be dead by now," Campbell said.

"We would be dead too," Jessie reminded him. "All of us, and not just Don Schaeffer. Friends help friends, James."

The half-breed said, "I wish I had a drink right now. But I must go."

"Be careful," said Jessie, aching at his departure but realizing that he was doing the right thing. "And when you get your medicine, come back—please."

Campbell looked at her, his dark eyes drinking her in. *"You* be careful, as well." And with that he was gone, moving as silently as a mountain cat, closing the door silently behind him.

Jessie said, "I fear for him, Ki. Somebody wants him dead, and they won't stop now."

"Do you have any idea who it is?" the samurai asked, ready to supply an answer himself.

Her emerald eyes sparkled in the lamplight as she sat cross-legged on the bed. "I have a suspicion, yes. And so do you. Mr. Lowell Henry. It's that simple. And yet it's not. How would Henry know that James is here to kill him? How would he know where James was staying? He must have spies everywhere."

"The man named Stella said his partner did some trading with the renegades in the desert. If Art French was working for Henry, then Henry must have dealings with the Apaches. He must be a very powerful man."

78

Jessie considered Ki's words. Undoubtedly, Henry *was* a powerful man in Las Cruces and in New Mexico Territory. He pulled a lot of strings and controlled many payrolls, probably—but would he stoop to hiring killers to eliminate someone like James Two Wolves Campbell? She had known many ruthless men for whom great wealth and power was never great enough, men who allowed nothing to hinder or inconvenience their ambition. If Lowell Henry fit this bill, then he would be very difficult—if not impossible—to contend with. If he could hire three men to kill Campbell tonight, he could hire three more or six more to try again tomorrow night, or the night after. Money would be no object until the job got done to his satisfaction.

"Did you find out anything tonight?" she asked Ki.

Ki reported his conversation with Horace Dunlop, the drunken drummer. "He told me that he thought it best to stay away from Henry. The man has a bad reputation."

"But that's no proof he tried to kill James."

"Dunlop said there have been many allegations—none proved conclusively, but enough for strong suspicions. Still, if Henry carries enough weight in Las Cruces, it's unlikely that he'll ever be challenged by anyone in town."

"It will take somebody from the outside—like James Campbell—to challenge him," Jessie said, her eyes alight. She brushed a hand through her thick red-gold hair. "If anyone can bring Henry down, it is James—with our help."

Ki cautioned her, "What about the Circle Star's business with Henry? We came here to sell him some cattle, remember. If he'll even talk to you after this."

"Maybe he won't tie me in with James right away," Jessie said. "Oh, I'll see him, and I'll talk to him—tomorrow, as planned. We'll talk plenty of business. I'll bargain with him over the cattle, let him think he's getting a real good deal." A plan was taking shape in her head. "I'll powwow with Henry—and I might even let him buy me dinner."

Shaking his head, Ki said, "Be careful, Jessie. Don't get

79

too cocky. Your father always used to warn you against that."

"I know, Ki. Don't go playing Alex Starbuck. You're too good at it."

The samurai felt battered and tired enough not to quarrel with her, but he would not let her go beard the lion without being prepared to pay the consequences. "Your father," he said, "made me promise to take care of you."

"I know—to save me from myself. Like a little girl playing with all the rough little boys. Well, I'm a grown woman now and—"

Ki smiled. "You keep reminding me of that, Jessie. I know it. I can see it for myself every time I look at you."

"You know you're right, don't you—damn it," she relented, the curse surprising even her. "It's just that—well, I hadn't expected any of this to happen. I thought we were riding to Las Cruces to sell beeves, not to get in the middle of somebody else's fight."

"The fight came to us yesterday. The renegade Apaches."

"We should have expected that," Jessie said. "They're everywhere, and the army only seems to make things worse by doing what they did to James's people."

"They're a proud race," Ki agreed. "A race of warriors, like the people of my homeland. They will not easily be herded onto bleak, waterless, lifeless reservations to die of hunger and hopelessness. Some, like these Mescaleros and Jicarillas, will fight, even against a general like Crook and against overwhelming numbers. It is their *bushido*, their honor."

"Yes," Jessie said. "And with such unrest throughout the territory, it's easy for unscrupulous white men to take advantage of the fears of the settlers and the plight of the desperate Indians, and make a handsome profit." She shook her head wearily. "There are always men willing to play both sides against each other. It's a dangerous game, but the stakes are high. If Lowell Henry is trading arms and whiskey to the Apache, he should face the stiffest penalty of law. And worse, if he sold that diseased meat to the reservation and killed all those people," she said angrily.

Ki said, "You should go back to bed, Jessie. And I must sleep. We have a lot to do in the morning."

"I'm sorry I brought you out here, Ki. I just didn't know. I should have checked into this deal more closely."

"We are here now. Nothing can change that. Perhaps we were meant to come here and encounter these people. My fighting skills need honing, as I found out this night."

"Good to keep in practice—is that what you're saying?" She laughed lightly.

"The gods will it. Who are we to dispute the gods?" He bowed formally to her. "Get some sleep, Jessie. Good night."

"Good night, Ki. And thank you." She blew out the lamp as Ki exited, and pulled her blanket up to her chin.

But sleep didn't come. Troubled thoughts kept her tossing and turning in bed. The image of her father, displeased with her, came to her in the darkness. He would probably administer a good spanking if he were here now.

She remembered his words to her just a few weeks before he died: "Jessie, you are blessed with your mother's beauty and intelligence, and cursed with your father's temper and stubbornness. Remember always to let your head govern your heart, or else you'll encounter as much trouble as I have in my life, which is too much trouble for anybody."

Jessie wanted to laugh and cry. A chill shivered up her spine. Her father was dead. All she had now were memories. She was a grown woman who had weathered many rough times with Ki at her side. It was time to put aside the girlish sadness over Alex Starbuck's death . . . but it was no use. The tears came despite her bitter self-recrimination.

She wept herself to sleep, worried about Ki and James Campbell and what the new day would bring.

Jessie dreamed that she was riding the range in the northwest quadrant of the vast Circle Star spread—that she was a girl again, with the wind blowing in her face as her horse galloped over the gullies that crisscrossed the West Texas earth. She was riding toward the distant mountains that jutted up blackly into the blue infinity of the sky. Her braids— for, when she was a little girl, she sometimes wore her shining hair in braids—flew like guidons behind her head as she sat low in the saddle and hugged her animal's neck. Then the sky grew dark and menacingly purple with swirling clouds, and she became cold. The sturdy horse, of the best Circle Star stock, galloped on, determined to bring his rider to the mountains, come what may. But only young Jessie could see that it was impossible to reach the mountains before the storm descended upon them. Impossible . . . yet she hugged her horse and urged him forward. The mountains beckoned her. And she rode on, expecting the rain to sheet down at any moment—which it never did . . .

Chapter 6

By day, the city came alive. The streets, lined with adobe structures, testified to the Spanish origin of Las Cruces: churches, homes, shops, and other buildings bore the imprint of that conquistador culture which had once ruled supreme in this part of the world. But the Americans had made their own stamp on the place by now, with frame and stone structures, including the local courthouse and many business offices, as well as saloons and hotels. The result was a babel of Spanish, American, and Indian tongues and tastes—a city that pulsated with life and, much of the time, danger. The people out on the sunblasted streets, their hats pulled low to escape the scorching rays, went about their well-defined jobs and kept out of each other's way and spoke mainly to their own people, mixing little with others.

Jessie struck out on her own that morning. Dressed in a fawn-colored riding skirt and a billowing white blouse with a lacy collar, she strode from her hotel room. Concealed in the bag slung over her shoulder was her converted .38 Colt revolver—just in case. She wore a broad-brimmed Stetson fastened by a leather cord beneath her chin, which did little to give her the anonymity she sought; for her golden-red hair was clearly visible as it hung almost to her shoulders. She could sense that, as she made her way to the center of town, she was the object of inquisitive looks from men and women she passed. But Jessie kept her gaze level, indicating that she would brook interference from no one.

After speaking to Ki over her morning coffee, she had decided she must meet Lowell Henry herself, alone, immediately, in order to feel the man out. Her pretext would, of course, be the proposed cattle deal.

Jessie hoped, above all, that James Two Wolves Campbell would keep his word and not attack Henry at least until she had had a chance to speak to the man. She worried about Campbell. For all his trail-toughness and demonstrated intelligence, she knew the man was driven by a burning need for vengeance. She could understand that; after all, her own father's death had been—and still was—such a cause for her. Yet Campbell was at a distinct disadvantage in his struggle. Any violent act on his part would bring the law down fast. If she could, she wanted to prevent that from happening.

Not knowing Henry, however, except from what Campbell and Ki had told her, she couldn't be sure what to expect from the man. That he was wealthy, that he was ruthless, that he pulled political strings with aplomb—of these things she was aware. But Lowell Henry the man was a stranger to her. Not for long, though.

She reached the center of town, near the large new courthouse in front of which a tall flagpole proudly displayed the Stars and Stripes. Jessie wondered how strong a hold the U.S. government could expect to maintain out here in this distant territory. With army troops at a premium these days, and hostile Indians roaming the desert, it was not an easy job—to say the least.

All of these thoughts ran through her mind as Jessie located the new two-story structure that housed Lowell Henry's business operation. Freshly whitewashed, the broad-fronted building had an expertly painted sign above the large front door: LOWELL HENRY, ESQ., ENTERPRISES. He certainly wasn't a bashful man, she noted wryly.

Inside, the building was clean and well lighted, with a dozen desks and three times as many file cabinets arranged around the floor. Each desk was manned by a busy-looking clerk. Near the front door a young woman sat behind a long, uncluttered desk and looked up brightly as Jessie entered. "May I help you?" the girl asked.

"Yes, I'm here to see Mr. Henry," said Jessie.

"Do you have an appointment?" the secretary inquired.

How many times have I heard that stupid question? Jessie wondered. It was as if all these girls were cut from the very same cloth. "No," she breathed. "But I have a letter from Mr. Henry, requesting me to drop in anytime, at my convenience. Please tell him I am here."

The girl looked over the letter. "Yes, Miss Starbuck," she replied cheerfully. With that, she wound her way to the back of the large room and into an office in the rear. She emerged a moment later and said to Jessie, "Mr. Henry will see you in just a few minutes. Would you like to take a seat?"

"No, thank you," Jessie said, preferring to stand and survey the impressive scene before her. Henry ran quite a smooth operation, it appeared. His enterprises generated a lot of paperwork, anyway. She paced impatiently to and fro; she did not like to be kept waiting in situations such as this.

A bell rang on the girl's desk. "That's him," she said. "He'll see you now." She led Jessie to the rear office and let her in, closing the big door behind her.

It was a spacious, high-ceilinged room, with heavy paneling on three walls and long bookshelves covering the entire fourth wall. The floor gleamed, its highly polished surface reflecting the light of a large chandelier that hung in the center of the office, above the massive desk. The sturdy, intricately carved maple desk took up nearly a quarter of the room by itself. And behind the desk, in a high-backed brown leather chair, sat Lowell Henry.

He rose and came to her, his hand outstretched. Henry was slightly shorter than average, trim, dressed expensively. His eyes were dark, almost black, set beneath an expansive forehead, and they drank in his guest. He wore a neatly trimmed brown mustache, and his firm jaw and prominent nose gave him a solid, not far from handsome face. His fingers were long and his nails manicured, Jessie noticed as she took his hand. His grip held her hand firmly. For a second she thought he was going to kiss her hand, but he did not, instead holding it for a moment and then releasing it.

"Welcome, Miss Starbuck. I am surprised and more than a little pleased to see you. I gather you received my letter and responded to my invitation."

His voice was low and even, his manner cultivated. Jessie found herself almost liking this charming, well-turned-out man. She guessed him to be in his mid-forties, and noticed that he carried not an ounce of excess weight, as men of his station and wealth usually did. He was fit and light on his feet. This was not the picture she had harbored of the man.

"I'll travel a long way to talk cattle, Mr. Henry. It is I who am grateful that you are interested in the Circle Star."

Lowell Henry pulled up two chairs in front of his desk. "Have a seat," he urged her. "Have you already eaten breakfast? I can have some food sent in. Or coffee?"

Jessie agreed to a cup of coffee, and Henry rang a small silver bell three times. Within a few seconds, a young man appeared with a pot of coffee and two cups on a silver tray. He poured the coffee and Henry passed Jessie her cup. It was a strong and delicious brew.

"This coffee is specially imported from Brazil," Henry remarked. "Well worth the expense."

"It is fine," Jessie said, wondering at the elaborate effort to impress her. She couldn't care less where Henry bought his coffee, though she had to admit it was delicious.

Henry sat easily opposite her, his eyes unwavering. She felt slightly uncomfortable under his frankly appraising gaze. Yet his attitude was not threatening or unfriendly. He said, "How did you travel? I hope you had a safe journey."

"On horseback," said Jessie. "One of the men from the ranch traveled with me." She decided to say nothing about the Apache attack, or about James Campbell. The less Henry knew about her, and her purpose here, the better.

"Dangerous," the man said, wrinkling his brow. "All the way from West Texas? That is some of the most treacherous country known to the white man. I'm doubly pleased you made it safely to Las Cruces." He kept his eyes locked on her face. He was clearly impressed with this young woman.

"Yes, we made it," she said simply. What did Henry know about how truly dangerous the desert was—and what trouble the Circle Star party might have encountered? "Not without some problems."

Henry raised a dark eyebrow. "Oh? What kind of problems?"

Jessie related an edited version of the story of the renegade attack—still without mentioning Campbell, or the fact that one of her men had been killed.

"You were lucky, Miss Starbuck," said Henry, when she had finished. "From what I gather, those roving Apache war parties are deadly. You are to be complimented on your skill and resourcefulness. I am happy you and your companion were unhurt."

Did he have any idea who her companion was? Had word of Ki's and Campbell's confrontation last night reached him? Something inside Jessie—a strong intuition—told her that Lowell Henry knew about everything that happened in and around Las Cruces. In fact, she considered it possible that Henry himself had instigated the attack on Campbell. But she had no evidence to substantiate this instinct. She'd have to ask some pointed questions of her own to uncover Henry's involvement, if any.

"As I told you, Mr. Henry, I am not afraid to face hardship in order to sell cattle." She formulated a plan as she spoke. "Let's get down to business. Are you planning to send a representative, or perhaps come yourself, to look over the Circle Star product?"

"I believe I can rely on your word, Miss Starbuck, that you raise some of the finest beef in the West." He removed a long, ribboned cigar from an inside pocket. "I frankly do not have the time for much traveling, nor can I spare any of my men presently."

"Will you be buying the beef for sale here in Las Cruces?" she went on.

"Well, I'm not certain at the moment, Miss Starbuck. You see, I do a lot of business with the government—supplying military outposts and Indian reservations. There is a great demand in both places for good meat."

"I imagine most traders sell inferior beef to the army and worse to the Indians. It's good to hear differently from you," she said.

Henry, lighting his cigar with a flaring match, flinched almost imperceptibly. No one but Jessie—who was looking for it—would have seen the slight, subtle reaction to her statement. Puffing now on the fragrant cigar, he said, "I take pride in keeping good relations with my customers, Miss Starbuck, be they white soldiers or redskins. They look to me for top-quality goods, and I make it my business to satisfy them."

Spoken like a seasoned businessman and politician, Jessie thought. But he wasn't telling the truth. She perceived a harder edge emerging in the man, a defensiveness that hadn't been there at first.

"I feel the same way," Jessie said. "The reputation of my family's business is very important to me."

"And a fine reputation it is," Henry commented smoothly. "I understand that your father, who founded the Starbuck company, died a while back. I'm sorry to hear that. He must have been quite a man."

"He was, Mr. Henry." It was her turn to be taken aback. Henry knew about Alex Starbuck? Of course, it shouldn't have been too surprising, for Starbuck's name had been legendary throughout the West. Still, it had been a long time now since his brutal assassination, and Jessie didn't expect that the killing had remained on people's minds for so long. So why had this man mentioned her father's death?

"It is unusual that he should have left the operations in the hands of a young woman," said Lowell Henry. "I do not doubt that you are capable, but you must agree it is unusual."

"I agree," Jessie replied. "Nonetheless, that is how it is."

Henry sensed her unease, saw her emerald eyes spark. "From my point of view, it is a pleasure to do business with such an attractive rancher," he said.

Jessie ignored the compliment. It had been tried before. She would not be flattered. "So you do intend to do business then?" she asked.

"Of course, my dear young lady. If we can come to acceptable terms." The man drew on his cigar, smoke streaming from his lips. One hand fingered the gold watch chain that hung from his vest pocket. Jessie noticed an expensive ruby ring on that hand. Henry had money to spare, all right, and he wasn't afraid to show the world.

"Well, what is your proposal, then?" she inquired. "What quantity are you interested in, and at what price?"

Henry chuckled. "I was hoping you would name the price. I want two thousand head, with an option on three thousand next year, if the quality is what you say it is."

89

Jessie said, "I wish to think about the price—for a while. Perhaps we can meet again tomorrow." She rose from her chair.

"Why put it off, Miss Starbuck? We could conclude the deal here and now, and then I'd be pleased to take you to lunch. What do you say?"

Jessie was confused. Henry's reputation as a hard-bargaining broker was belied by his agreeable attitude this morning. She had expected drawn-out negotiations over the price, but he was already asking her to name a figure! It didn't make sense, according to what she had heard about the man. And she was reluctant to close a deal with him so quickly. She didn't yet know enough about him to trust him, despite his open manner.

She sat down again, and smiled. She would have to use all her wiles with Henry. "Frankly," Jessie said, "I expected a tougher time making this deal, Mr. Henry. I could name any price—and you'd accept it?"

"Not necessarily. But, you see, I fully expect you to be reasonable. You want to sell, and I want to buy." His tone was low and measured. He kept that smile on his face and exuded sincerity. He seemed to enjoy dealing with a pretty young woman.

Jessie stated a price, well above the current market figure but not sky-high.

Henry exhaled smoke and considered his cigar. "This tobacco I buy from Cuba," he said matter-of-factly. "I pay a premium price, willingly. Let's talk about your price over lunch, Miss Starbuck."

Now it was Jessie's turn to smile. Damn the man, but he had charm. Was he really capable of switching diseased meat with good and sending scores of innocent people to their deaths? *Well,* she decided, *I'll have to let him hang himself if it's true.*

"Yes, lunch is a good idea," she said.

Lowell Henry took Jessie to a nearby eating place— presumably the most expensive in town. He drank cold

Mexican beer with his meal, and Jessie enjoyed a glass of smooth red wine—imported, she had no doubt. During lunch she learned much about Henry's background—or at least as much as he wanted her to know. Clearly, it gave him pleasure to recount his life story to this girl. In the flickering light within the dark, cavernous restaurant, her face and hair glowed alluringly.

He had come from Ohio originally, served in the Union army as a youth, and drifted west after the war, determined to make his fortune. He had wound up in Sacramento, California, where he worked in a bank, rising to the rank of vice-president within three years.

"Then I had to make a choice," he said. "I could stay there and become president of the bank one day, or else strike out on my own again and be my own boss." He shrugged his shoulders. "It really wasn't much of a choice. I worked in Sacramento for another year, saving my money, and then came here, to Las Cruces, where I knew some people, and set up my own business."

Jessie listened impassively, uncertain as to why Henry was telling her all of this—unless to lull her into feeling that she was being taken fully into his confidence.

Henry described how he had turned his original investment into a profit within a year and gone on to build an ever-increasing operation that included mining, cattle, and bank interests, and held mortgages throughout the city and in neighboring towns. He seemed well pleased with his success so far, and said nothing that would betray even a hint of dirty dealings along the way.

Jessie stored away the facts as he related them. She would use them, if necessary, to check on Lowell Henry—to verify his version of events. But she still wanted to know more about his dealings with the Indians, both the sale of meat and other goods to reservations and the illegal trade of guns and whiskey to renegade bands like the one that had attacked her party.

She said, "Didn't you pick a particularly dangerous part

91

of the territory to set up your business in?"

"The greater the risk, the greater the potential reward," Henry said. "I do not fear these renegade Indians. I trust that the army will see to it that they are subdued very soon."

"But as long as the Indians have access to illegal arms and ammunition—won't they be a threat?" Here was the core of her question, and she watched Henry's reaction closely.

His dark eyes bored into her and he paused before answering. "It is the army's job to keep weapons and liquor from the Indians. We civilians can only do our best to see that supplies do not fall into the hands of our more unscrupulous brethren. Do you know something about this activity, Miss Starbuck? If so, I urge you to speak with the appropriate legal or military officials." He pushed away his plate and lit another cigar.

"I have nothing specific. Only suspicions," Jessie said.

"I see," Henry grunted noncommittally. He concentrated on applying the match flame to his cigar.

Jessie decided to probe a little deeper. "I've heard rumors, Mr. Henry, that disturb me greatly. One story has it that a diseased beef shipment was diverted to an Indian reservation up north, killing a large number of innocent Indians."

"Well, I'm afraid there is corruption everywhere, my dear Miss Starbuck. I try to keep a tight rein on my own people, but others, I'm afraid, are not so scrupulous. And what else have you heard?" Despite his casual tone, Jessie sensed that she was upsetting him.

"When we were riding into town, my companion and me, we found sign of a meeting between Apaches and white men. It looked like a drop-off point—we guessed for guns or liquor, or both. We followed the wagon trial, and it led us right back to Las Cruces."

Henry lifted his hands. "I am not surprised, but I have no idea who might be involved in such dealings. As I said,

I can only control those who work directly for me."

"It must be a profitable business—dealing with the renegades, I mean."

"Undoubtedly," Henry agreed. "But the risks are far too great for any intelligent man to assume. These traders are petty thieves and smugglers. I hope the law finds them and punishes them."

Commendable public spirit, Jessie mused ironically. He was, of course, going to admit nothing—if he knew anything. She reminded herself that nothing had been proved; she had only James Campbell's accusation and other circumstantial evidence to go on.

She decided to play another card. "My companion was involved in an unfortunate incident last night. Perhaps you heard about it. A couple of men were killed. My companion came to the aid of another man who was being attacked. Is this kind of violence common here in Las Cruces?"

This time Lowell Henry's temper flared. "This city is generally a very peaceful place to live and work, Miss Starbuck. When troublemakers from out of town try to stir things up, there's very little we can do to stop them. I only hope your friend had good reason to involve himself. Yes, I heard about it. There is very little in Las Cruces that I do not hear about," he said evenly, his eyes locked on hers. She could see the muscles at his temples tighten. She had hit home with that one.

"Well, according to my friend, the attack was unprovoked. The man—an Indian, I think—was in his room when three men burst in, aiming to kill him. Ki did the right thing and helped the man fight them off. I would have done the same."

"You're a brave girl," said Henry. "But if I were you, I wouldn't get involved in such matters. From what I hear, this Indian—or half-breed, more properly—is one of those troubleseekers I alluded to. We do not appreciate his kind in this town."

"Oh, so you've heard of the man?" Jessie inquired as innocently as she could.

"This is what I was *told* by my sources. A man in my position must have eyes and ears everywhere, Miss Starbuck."

"Yes, I suppose you must." This was what she had wanted, to put Henry on the defensive.

"I am very glad you agreed to dine with me," he said. "This has been an enlightening discussion."

"Don't you want to discuss the price I proposed earlier?"

"I'm afraid I must get back to the office. We can talk further tomorrow."

"Very well," Jessie said, secretly pleased that he was disturbed enough not to want to continue with their business of the morning.

Henry rose from his chair, clutching his burning cigar. "Good day, Miss Starbuck. I really cannot linger here any longer. If you'll pardon me."

"Thank you for the delicious meal, Mr. Henry," she replied. "I'll call on you tomorrow."

She watched him leave, apprehension growing in her gut. Had she said too much? Been too inquisitive? Pushed him too far? Time would tell. She just prayed that James Campbell would return to her unharmed—and that the three of them could face whatever Henry threw at them.

• • •

At noon, Ki returned to the saloon where, the night before, he had met the girl Rita. He hoped to run into Dunlop again, as well. If he could catch the man at a more sober stage in his day, perhaps Dunlop could tell him more about Henry.

The drummer was nowhere to be seen, however, so Ki went to the bar and ordered a beer to nurse. He planned to wait an hour or so, to give Dunlop a chance to show up. Several minutes later he saw Rita instead.

The girl came up to Ki, her beautiful dark face clouded with sadness. She was dressed in her "working clothes," a low-cut blouse that hugged her high breasts, a bright blue and red skirt, dark stockings, and high-heeled laced shoes. Her long black hair was combed back and held in place by a red ribbon. His heart went out to her.

"Hello, Ki," Rita said quietly.

"What is wrong, Rita?" he asked, lifting her face with a gentle hand beneath her chin.

"I am afraid," she said, her voice falling to a whisper.

"Why? What have you done?"

"Nothing. Except to be with you," she replied.

"With me? What's wrong with that? Has someone threatened you, Rita? Tell me."

The girl swallowed hard, trying to keep the tears from flowing. "I am such a weak, stupid girl," she said. "I cry at everything."

Ki managed a smile, trying to reassure her. "Don't say that. You are a strong girl."

She took a small envelope from the waistband of her skirt.

"Ki, I found this slipped under my door this morning. It is addressed to you. I am frightened. Whoever it is knows you were with me last night."

The samurai took the envelope from Rita. For a fleeting moment he was sorry he had involved her—however unwittingly—in his business in Las Cruces. Already it had turned out to be an extremely dangerous situation. He did not want to see the girl hurt, at any cost.

He put a hand on her shoulder. "Don't be frightened. I'll see that no harm comes to you," he promised. "Perhaps it would be better if we weren't seen together again. I will leave here now and return to my hotel. If you need me, you can find me there—or leave a message." He gave her the name of the hotel, and his room number. "But don't be afraid, Rita, please."

95

"Yes, Ki," she said, blinking back the tears.

Ki returned to his hotel and opened the envelope. Inside was a letter—from Horace Dunlop.

Dear Mr. Ki,

I have taken the unusual step of writing you, instead of speaking to you directly, because I am leaving town posthaste. The reason I am departing so unexpectedly is that I value my own skin. Let me explain.

Although I was—how to say it?—inebriated last night, I remember everything we talked about, and your kind help in seeing me to my room (for which I thank you). I should have realized, however, that everything that passed between us was heard by others at the bar—including at least one man who is paid to eavesdrop on such conversations by none other than Mr. Lowell Henry, the subject of our discussion. This man visited me less than an hour ago and told me, as he checked the loads in his revolver, to return to Kansas City and forget about returning to Las Cruces in the future. I took him at his word, and by the time you read this I shall be on the train.

I sense that you—if you choose to remain—are in more danger than you may realize. So I would advise you, too, to leave. Something, though, tells me that your business is important enough to compel you to stay. If such is the case, let me advise you, in all sobriety, to be very careful in your inquiries concerning Mr. Lowell Henry.

Everything I told you last night was true. I have made it my concern to find out about the man, in hopes of doing business with him. That was never to be, but I did discover certain unsavory allegations against the man. He holds practically the entire city under his thumb, politically and financially. No one dares challenge his authority, even though he is not so brutal as to be directly involved with reprisals against his enemies. Hired men take care of that dirty work. And, I am told—and this is the most startling part of the story—Henry has direct links to the renegade Apaches, through the gun and whiskey trade, and sometimes uses their services to quiet his opponents! As preposterous as this sounds, I have a reliable source for such information. Perhaps you should speak with him. His name is Willis. He is an employee in Mr. Henry's office. He seems to have a personal grudge against Henry, for what reason I do not know.

Whether or not you reach this man, let me repeat to you, Mr. Ki, that you must use the utmost caution—for anything concerning Henry's dealings is potentially explosive. I never fancied getting blown up, which is why I'm long gone.

One final matter: I am enclosing a draft for fifty dollars, payable at the issuing bank. This is for Señorita Rita. I am not a rich man, or else I would have taken her with me and helped her start a new life away from there. Instead, I am giving her this money in the hope that it may help her escape her present condition. Also, I beg that you send her my warmest regards in addition to the money.

I felt, after last night, that I was in your debt, Mr. Ki. Hence this missive. Please heed my warning, and with it accept my best wishes for your success.

Your humble servant,
Horace Dunlop

Ki reread the letter. An extraordinary document, he thought. He had underestimated Dunlop. He pocketed the bank note; he would give it to the girl later. First he would seek out this man named Willis who worked for Lowell Henry. He knew Jessie was meeting with the businessman this morning. He went to her room and knocked on the door. There was no answer. It was almost one o'clock. He went back to his room to wait for her.

Only a few minutes later, Jessie returned. She stopped by Ki's room before going to hers. He showed her the letter.

Jessie read Dunlop's note with growing unease. She turned to Ki. "I wonder who this Willis is, and how much he knows."

"I mean to find out, Jessie."

"Ki, I wish we hadn't ridden into this whole mess. We should be back at the Circle Star, preparing for the fall roundup."

"Now that we are here, we must see the matter to a conclusion."

Jessie sighed. She told Ki of her talk with Henry—and how he had impressed her as a very slick, shrewd, self-possessed man. He would be a formidable enemy if they took him on by themselves. Then it struck her. "Perhaps we should notify the territorial authorities of the allegations against Henry. No doubt he has his friends in the government, but if we could get around them..."

"Didn't your father know General Lew Wallace, the governor?"

Jessie said, "Yes. He admired Wallace's military reputation. He said the general is also a fine writer. He often wished Wallace would write a book."

"For now we must alert him to the situation here."

"For my father's sake, I hope the governor takes an interest," she said.

★

Chapter 7

It was late. Jessie felt the four walls of the hotel room penning her in as she talked with Ki. Though the town was quiet, there was violence in the air. The letter from Horace Dunlop made that clear—just as her meeting with Lowell Henry had brought the fact home to her. If she called on Governor Wallace, however, she would need hard facts, not merely vague allegations.

A quiet knock at her door startled Jessie. She and Ki sprang upright, Jessie with her .38 Colt in her hand, Ki drawing his *tanto* blade. The coal oil lamp flickered at their movement, sending their shadows dancing like ghosts on the wall.

"Who's there?" Jessie called.

"Two Wolves," came the reply.

Relieved, Jessie let Campbell in "Hello, James," she said. "I'm glad it's you."

James Two Wolves Campbell stepped into the room. He looked from Jessie to Ki. "Were you expecting other visitors?" he asked.

Jessie laughed lightly. "We weren't expecting anybody. But it's good to see you."

Ki, too, was relieved to see the half-breed. He replaced his weapon in its lacquered sheath at his waist.

Jessie said, "Sit down, James. Tell us about your journey to the desert."

Campbell looked haggard, the lines in his face deeper, the scar more livid, his eyes sunken. It was apparent he had eaten nothing and probably drunk nothing but water for the past twenty-four hours. He sat on the end of Jessie's bed, facing her. "There is little to tell. I went to strengthen my medicine, to look for a sign."

Jessie studied the handsome half-breed. Something had happened to him out there in the desert; she was not certain what, but she could tell by his slightly stooped posture and drawn features that he had discovered something that bothered him greatly. She wanted to pepper him with questions, to comfort him in her arms, to learn what was really going through his mind. But she waited instead for him to speak, to put the experience into words.

"I went to the desert, walking for miles. I don't know how many miles—perhaps fifteen. I walked until dawn and then I waited as the sun rose above the mountains. As I waited, I smoked some sumac mixed with tobacco in an old pipe my grandfather gave me. I sat on the hard desert earth and felt it warm beneath me as the night went away. And as I smoked, I called on the spirits of the earth to tell me what I wanted to know, to give me a sign of that which is to come.

"My prayers were answered. I saw a great wolf in the distance and rose to follow him. The wolf is my medicine; I was named for him. This animal was a large one—bigger than some mountain cats I have seen. He led me toward the foothills, sometimes disappearing, sometimes appearing just a few yards ahead of me. I kept following him. I knew he was leading me to a vision of the truth, that he was sent to teach me what I wanted to know."

The half-breed spoke with reverence of the experience. He had never forgotten his training as a Comanche, even through years of living among white men. "I went into the hills," he continued, "hungry and thirsty, but daring not to stop, my senses keen to every sight and smell and sound— like the wolf's."

Jessie and Ki listened intently to Campbell's every word. They knew that the man could not relate the essence of his mystical search in mere words. But he was telling them what he could—in words they would understand.

"The wolf, after taking me on a long journey toward the base of the mountains, then turned and looked at me. His eyes glowed like the sun and he opened his mouth in a silent howl, his jagged teeth exposed as he drew back his lips. It seemed that he was speaking to me, and I struggled to understand what he said. And then it came to me: 'My brother,' he said, 'you are right to fight against evil. But this battle is not for you to win.' Without speaking the words, I asked him why this was to be. He said, 'It is the will of the Great Spirit who rules us all. You have fought many battles and done much good in your lifetime. None of us lives forever in the flesh; only the spirits of good and evil live forever among men.' The he turned and began to walk away from me. He let out a long howl, and then he vanished. I did not see him again. I began to walk back the way I came."

Jessie felt a painful pressure in her heart. She did not like to hear him speak this way—it sounded fatalistic, as if he had accepted his own death.

Campbell went on, "As I made my way through the hills, I came upon a cave. Something inside me told me to go into the cave, and so I did. There I found a strange thing.

On the floor of the cave were the remains of an eagle and a snake. How they got there I do not know—but they were locked in battle, the eagle's beak biting into the snake and the snake's tail wrapped around the eagle's body, pinning its wings. Both were dead. Neither of them had given up the fight, and both had lost. I have never seen such a thing in my life. It was an omen of death. As I walked back through the desert I tried to understand what they meant, these things I was shown. It took me many hours to find my way back to the city. I had time to think and pray. I know now what the wolf was trying to tell me: I must not try to kill Lowell Henry for what he has done; I must trust to the white man's justice. If I pursue him, it has to be through the court system. I cannot win by fighting him in the only way I know how."

"How do you propose to bring charges against Henry?" Jessie asked. "Ki and I will help you in any way we can. You have to be careful, though, James. I'm worried that—" She could not finish her thought. Campbell's story disturbed her greatly, and she felt that he wasn't telling everything he had found out.

"What are you saying?" Campbell asked her.

"I don't know. It's just that what you saw out there—it doesn't sound like good medicine."

The half-breed shook his head. "It is not, Jessie. The eagle and the snake—they represent the struggle we are engaged in, and they mean that neither side will win. I expect that the omen also means I am marked for death."

"No!" exclaimed Jessie in a strangled cry. She could not—did not want to—believe that this was true. In the short time she had known him, James Campbell had come to mean a lot to her.

Ki, who had stood by listening to Campbell's story, also felt a twinge of regret at the half-breed's conclusions. Yet he understood how and why Campbell had arrived at the unmistakable meaning of those signs. Ki, too, had a mystical element in his makeup—as all good warriors do. Still, he

102

held on to the hope that it wasn't true, that the big man who had led their fight against the renegade Apaches would be with them for a long time to come.

Campbell reached out and touched Jessie's hand. "Do not deny the will of the gods. No matter what we do, the spirits that rule this world will prevail. It is not bad, it is simply the way things are."

"But I don't want you to die, James. I don't want to lose you."

"I am not afraid to die, if I must."

"That's not what I mean," Jessie pleaded. "Why do you have to die just because you found some dead animals in a cave? There can be other meanings, can't there? And if you fight Henry in the courts, instead of trying to kill him, won't that diminish the danger you face?"

"However I fight Henry, he will want to kill me, to get me out of the way. It is simply the way he is. Surely you have not found out differently, have you?"

Jessie told Campbell of her meeting with Lowell Henry that morning. Despite his attempt to play the disinterested businessman, she had sensed some unpleasant aspects of Henry's character—which were described in more detail in Dunlop's mysterious letter. She gave Campbell the letter to read for himself.

Campbell said, "We must talk to this man Willis—find out just how much he knows."

Jessie glanced over at Ki, worry scoring her face. She turned again to the half-breed. "You shouldn't talk to anyone. You have to stay out of sight, James. Let Ki and me take care of this."

Campbell said, "I have nothing to fear, Jessie. My life is worth nothing as long as Henry is a free man. I must accept that. But I must also do everything I can to see him put in jail."

"Then you *are* going to the law with your charges?" She was torn between relief and fear.

"It is the right way—whether I win or not, whether I

live or die. That is what I learned in the desert. Henry must be punished for his deeds."

"I hope we can find out from Willis what Henry has done, where to dig up the evidence. Ki," she added, "we will go talk to him tomorrow, you and I."

Ki nodded. "We must speak to him privately. No one can know what we are doing."

Jessie agreed, but wondered how extensive Henry's sources of information really were—whether he would know they had seen Willis, no matter how cautiously they arranged a meeting.

Then Ki excused himself and returned to his own room to ponder the situation before he slept.

Campbell remained where he was, seated on the bed, as Jessie let Ki out. He watched her as she came back to the bed and sat near him. Her lovely green eyes were bright, her skin glowing, her lips parted as if to speak. She said nothing, but kissed him instead.

"I'm so glad you're back safely—alive," she breathed as she pulled away from him. "I worried about you, James."

"I am back, yes, and alive for now. I wanted to see you again, too. I thought much about you when I was out in the desert. I had to return to stand at your side."

"I don't like it when you talk about dying, James. We're all going to come out of this fine, including you. Henry may throw his guns at us before it's over with, but we'll give back as good as we get. He won't beat us this time."

"The wolf told me this battle is not mine to win, Jessie. I believe him, for he speaks with the authority of the gods. It's not something I fear, it's just the way things are."

"Well, I don't like it," she said. "And I'm not going to let them kill you." She paused, gazing into his eyes. "You mean too much to me," she added, fighting back the tears. No, she would not give in to the feminine urge to cry— what she needed now was all the strength she possessed.

They had known each other for such a short time, and so few words had been exchanged between them, yet they now held a common purpose and were threatened by a common danger, and Jessie felt a strong bond between herself and this dark, quietly intense man.

"Jessie, whatever happens, I will always be with you. You are a beautiful and proud woman, and you give me strength when you are with me—as a woman should. My grief over the deaths of my mother and many of her people is strong, but my need for you is just as strong."

As he put his arms around her, Jessie's mind reeled. She needed this man, too. His strength and courage touched a part of her deep within herself, and she longed to have him with her always—if only that were possible. His powerfully muscled arms enfolded her securely and eased her troubled thoughts. At least for tonight she had this man, and for that she was grateful.

She lifted her face to his, and their lips met. They kissed long and hard, Jessie wrapping her arms around his back, holding him to her. She didn't want to let him go.

Campbell's tongue darted into her open mouth and Jessie responded eagerly, a flame flaring at the very core of her being. She crushed her lips to his and fought his tongue with her own, tasting the desert rawness of him, answering his urgency with her own. She kept her eyes closed tightly, living this moment as if it were a dream that would never end. *God,* she prayed silently, *please don't let anything happen to him . . .*

Campbell eased her down on the bed, embracing her gently. His handsome, deeply lined face hung above hers and he kissed her again, softly this time. Running his tongue over her lips and then between her teeth, he explored her hungry mouth, teasing her at the same time. He was in no hurry, though he wanted her badly. She savored him, her breasts crushed against his broad chest as he lay atop her.

The dirty golden light from the coal oil lamp flickered, the shadows wavering on the walls. Jessie whispered, "Let's put out the light, James."

He went to the lamp and extinguished the flame, flooding

the room in darkness. He returned to her and joined her in the bed. He lay alongside her and placed a hand on one breast that rose and fell as she breathed. Jessie stroked his long hair and ran her hand down over his muscled shoulders.

"James," she murmured, "why must we live like this—always flirting with death, when we could find peace together? Maybe we should go away tomorrow, leave this place."

Campbell said, "We were born to this life, Jessie. We were born to fight our enemies and to avenge the injustices suffered by our parents. We cannot go away from here. The only escape is death."

Jessie propped herself up on her elbows. She knew that what he said was true. She was now involved in Campbell's fight; it had become her own, and she must see it through. But she was angry that he insisted on talking of death. "I want you to stop that talk right now, or else I'll throw you out," she said. "We'll stay right here until it's over."

"You are a strange woman," the half-breed said. "If you were a Comanche, you would be the mother of warriors, a woman like Quanah Parker's mother. I wish I had known you long ago, that you could be the mother of my sons."

"That's an unusual proposal for marriage," Jessie joked. "I have much to do before I settle down and have sons."

Secretly, she was flattered. She wondered what it would have been like to live among the Comanches when they rode the plains as free as the wind, when they battled their enemies or hunted the buffalo. If she had met James Two Wolves Campbell years ago, if she had been old enough then . . . what would her father have said about such a match? A smile curled her full lips. What an enigma this man Campbell was!

"Don't you have any children, James?" she asked.

"No," he said simply. "I have not known the right woman. Not until now."

Silence descended on the pair as they lay in her bed. A

soft breeze washed into the room through an open window. She stroked his hair again. He breathed in her fragrance. Then he reached over and began to unfasten her blouse. Jessie let him. He opened it and put his hand inside, touching her already aroused breasts, running his fingers lightly over the fine, taut nipples. Jessie sighed and felt a shiver course through her body.

She pulled his head over and offered her breasts to him. Campbell flicked his tongue over her creamy globes and bit gently at the nipples with his strong white teeth.

Jessie moaned and held him there, enjoying the excitement he created within her, wanting more and more. Campbell sucked on her breasts and ran his hand down over her flat stomach. She still wore her riding skirt. Campbell helped her slip the skirt off and remove her boots and undergarments.

Within a few moments she lay there naked before him, and the man drank in the sight: her shining red-gold hair and fresh white skin that seemed to glow despite the lack of light; her round, perfect breasts; the long legs that seemed to belong on a marble statue, so perfect were they.

Campbell then undressed himself, removing his shirt, buckskin pants, and moccasins, placing his revolver and knife on the small table at the head of the bed, within easy reach. Jessie felt his lithe, lean body against hers as he came to her.

Hotly they clung together, exploring and admiring each other. Campbell's big hand cupped Jessie's buttocks. Jessie, in turn, raked her fingers up and down his back, and kissed him hungrily. Each experienced an overpowering need for the other—an unspoken command to please, and to take the love that was given in return.

Jessie could no longer resist the urge. She freed herself from his strong grasp and began kissing him, moving her lips from his face to the hollow of his neck and across the big shoulders, down to his wide chest, lingering on his dark nipples with her teeth. She brushed her lips down over his taut, flat stomach, and reaching with both her mouth and her hand, she discovered the powerful, erect manhood that testified to his need for her.

"Woman," Campbell breathed, "what are you doing?"

"I will show you how I have learned to love a man, how I can please him and make him rage with desire."

With that, she began teasing him with her tongue. She wanted to make the best use of the techniques her father's housekeeper and her teacher, the Japanese woman Myobu, had taught her. The Oriental ways of love were more un-inhibited than Western ways, and Jessie had learned those liberating techniques. She wanted to share them with James Campbell and bring him to as intense and enjoyable an orgasm as was possible.

Jessie opened her mouth and swallowed as much of him as she could manage. His blood-engorged weapon was im-mense, and she worked her hand up and down its length as she tasted it. It was a beautiful sensation, for Jessie and for Campbell. For her it was a new way to satisfy him, to heighten his pleasure; for him it was something he had never encountered, as this beautiful girl with the shining hair made love to him in this unique manner.

"Oh, Jessie—girl—" the big half-breed groaned. His eyes were shut tight, and beads of perspiration rolled down his forehead.

Jessie's head rose and fell and her hand pumped as she stroked his sword, bringing him very close to the edge before she stopped.

Still grasping his manhood tightly, she pulled herself up beside him. His dark face was a mask of exquisite longing. "Where—where did you learn to do that?" he asked.

Jessie laughed quietly. "A Japanese woman taught me the many ways of love when I was a young girl. She told me that it was highly honorable to please the man you love. I want to please you, James."

Campbell took her face in his hands and kissed her hard. "You learned well, Jessie," he said with a smile. Then he lifted her and laid her down on the bed on her back and climbed on top of her, his knees straddling her hips.

Jessie had to let go of his erection as he positioned himself. She looked up and saw his long figure above her, a shadow of a godlike man, and she felt the heat from his body as he came down on top of her. She opened her legs to him, and Campbell shifted so that he was poised at her gate.

He bent to kiss her, and as he did so he reached down past the soft thatch of hair on her mound, and touched the tender, moistened lips between her legs. His finger probed gently and he found that she was ready for him. Unable to contain himself any longer, the half-breed was ready to enter her. He gazed down at Jessie's beautiful face in the darkness, and saw her gleaming white teeth and bright eyes open in anticipation.

She found his stiff shaft and guided him home. Jessie gave out a cry, half pain and half delight, as she took his entire length inside her. She lifted her legs and joined her ankles around the small of his back as he began pumping steadily.

Jessie became all hot and liquid as her lover plunged his sword into her willing sheath. It was a feeling that possessed her entire body as she felt his strength inside her; she was like a languid beach upon which the sea pounded with relentless force, washing away any resistance, leveling everything in its path.

"James, please—yes, please love me. I want you—all of you—oh, yes!" she cried.

Campbell could not speak. He thrust harder, then relaxed and slid in and out at a slower pace, helping her to build toward climax. He himself could hardly hold back, but he did, wanting to make this moment last as long as possible. He had never felt himself aroused like this before, and he

109

did not want it to end. The beautiful girl beneath him squirmed and bucked with every plunge.

As he rotated his hips, increasing his penetration even further, Jessie moaned in ecstasy. She wanted him even deeper! So she lifted her pelvis to meet his strokes. Her legs remained locked around his back and she gripped his shoulders with all her strength.

Through gritted teeth, Campbell said, "That's it, girl . . . that's the way."

The bed groaned and creaked beneath them as they increased the pace of their lovemaking. But neither of them took notice, so involved were they in the rhythm of their own bodies. Campbell then rode harder, increasing the power of his thrusts into her open chamber, and Jessie responded eagerly. She reached down to grasp his lean buttocks and squeeze them, pulling him into her. The half-breed plunged home again and again, causing Jessie to struggle for every breath.

"God, James! It's so good like this!" She could barely contain herself now. Sweat trickled down her face and she felt the slickness of his body, too, against hers. "That's the way—yes! Please give it to me, James, please!"

Campbell needed no encouragement, for he was completely absorbed in his task, bulling her with everything he had. Her breasts rose to meet his chest and he felt the erect nipples grazing his flesh and nothing could stop him now. He thrust into her repeatedly, losing himself totally in her arms.

Jessie was at the brink. The heat that had built up between them threatened to melt her, and her silken thighs moved against Campbell's hard hips. Gasping for air, moving to meet his long strokes, she fought the impending explosion. She wanted it to last forever, but knew it could not. The half-breed's big weapon was splitting her in two.

He also was near climax, and realized that he was driving her closer and closer. Almost uncontrollably, he began pumping faster and faster. There was nothing left to lose now. He would give her everything. Her legs quivered as he drove his sword in relentlessly. Then it happened.

"James, James!" Jessie thrashed, tossing her head from side to side on the bed. From the core of her sex she felt the rippling effect of her orgasm build, then flash like lightning throughout her entire body. It weakened her, yet infused her with strength. Her eyes closed tightly, she could see white and blue lights igniting, fading, then exploding once again. Then she went liquid.

She cried out again, "Oh, James, you've done it to me, darling..."

At the same moment, Campbell fell over the precipice as he gave her his last ounce of pounding strength. His liquid essence exploded from him, shooting into her dark cave, filling her up and draining him. Again and again it spurted from him, until there was no more left, and he collapsed upon her.

Jessie wrapped her arms around the big man, feeling his erection still within her secret chamber. This was what she had always longed for—a strong but tender lover who was not afraid to give all of himself to her.

"James, James," she whispered, cradling his head in her hands.

Campbell was silent for a moment, breathing heavily, and then he said, "You have taken this warrior's strength and given him back even more. You are good for a man, Jessie."

"I want to be good—for one particular man. I'm glad we—I mean, I wanted you so much, James. I can't tell you how much."

He kissed her, their lips crushing together wetly. Her hair was damp from their passionate lovemaking. In the darkness he smiled. This was a special kind of woman, unlike any he had ever met before.

Jessie held him in silence as both felt the glow that comes

111

from an overwhelming sexual encounter. She wished she could keep him with her like this always. If only the rest of the world would not interfere—if they were different people—which was an impossibility. She ran her hands across his shoulder blades, admiring yet again his marvelous, strong body.

"Will you stay the night with me, James?" she asked him.

"Yes, if that is what you want," said Campbell. He stroked her richly burnished golden hair.

"What do you think will happen to us?" The trembling in her voice surprised even Jessie.

"I do not wish to think of that," he replied. "It is not for us to know. We must only do what we can. My vision—" He cut off the thought. "I only know what I saw in the desert, Jessie."

Saddened, but determined not to let him go, she said, "I believe you had the vision you told us about. But you also said that you would fight your battle in the territorial courts, rather than trying to kill Henry. I want to help you fight that battle. And I think we *can* win. You talk as if you have no future. I don't want to hear that from you."

"I only speak what I know. And I heard the wolf, my brother, tell me that this battle is not for me to win. But I will fight it—with you."

"James, you are a stubborn man," she said. "Are all the Comanche men stubborn like you?"

"They are bull-headed, yes. But the Boston people, on my father's side, are the most stubborn men you will ever meet. Perhaps I am too much like them, after all."

Jessie laughed. She was fighting tears. She had cried too much already on this journey—and she was determined to contain her female weakness. "I can believe that," she told him. "Stubborn Yankee blood mixed with Comanche. A deadly combination."

"You have to take me for what I am," he reminded her.

112

"Oh, I have no problem with that, James. I like what you are—every bit of you." As she spoke, she reached down to locate his flaccid manhood. The organ sprang to life at her touch.

"Woman, I shall die in your bed if you continue to do this to me. But it is a good place to die."

Chapter 8

When she awoke the next day, Jessie found that Campbell had gone. She bathed and dressed and went to Ki's room and found the samurai there waiting for her. He had been up early and out, looking into the situation of the man named Willis. What he had found out disturbed him. "Willis quit his job yesterday," he told Jessie. "He bought a ticket on the westbound stage that leaves tomorrow. If we want to talk to him, we'll have to find him today."

"Where does he live?" she asked.

"Not too far from here, in a boarding house," Ki replied.

"Let's go," Jessie said. She curbed the impulse to look in on James Campbell. First things first. And Willis was the first thing this morning.

Jessie and Ki found the boardinghouse without trouble. It was a neat, two-story affair sitting between two adobe structures, a saloon and a smithy. Ki told Jessie that Dunlop had once stayed here, which was how he knew of Willis. The house was run by a Mrs. Fielding, described by a man Ki had talked to as "a good Christian woman."

A woman in her fifties, her silver hair pulled back in a tight bun, a flowered apron around her ample waist, came to the door. She took in her two visitors with a glance: Jessie in a clean blouse and skirt, Ki in his open-necked cotton shirt, denim pants, and rope-soled footwear. "May I help you?" she asked tentatively.

"Are you Mrs. Fielding?" Jessie inquired.

"Yes," said the woman. "And who might you be?"

Jessie introduced herself and Ki. "We wish to speak to one of your boarders, ma'am. Mr. Willis. It's important business."

Mrs. Fielding considered Jessie's request. She eyed the pair suspiciously. Obviously a cautious woman, protective of her boarders, she was reluctant to invite Jessie and Ki inside.

"What kind of business?" she asked.

"I realize that you don't know us, Mrs. Fielding. But you must trust me. I will not cause trouble for you or Mr. Willis. I simply must talk to him before he leaves Las Cruces."

"So you know he is leaving town," the woman said. "What else do you know? You are not law officers, and you have no right to come into my house and cause a disturbance."

"As I said," Jessie went on, "we do not wish to make trouble, ma'am. We aren't law officers, but it won't be long before the law will want to talk to Mr. Willis."

"Why? What has he done?"

"Nothing," Jessie said. "But he may know about certain illegal activities. That is what we want to talk to him about."

Still wary, not quite convinced, the woman said, "Well, I'll let you see him in the parlor. I do not like to allow strangers into my house. And Mr. Willis is a nice man,

116

never a problem like some. He's always paid for his room and board on time and respected the privacy of others. I owe him that respect in return."

"I appreciate that, Mrs. Fielding," said Jessie. "I promise you we won't create a disturbance."

Mrs. Fielding said, "I'll tell Mr. Willis you are here. You'll wait in the parlor?"

"Thank you," Jessie said, and she and Ki followed the woman inside.

They waited for ten minutes in a pleasantly appointed sitting room. Mrs. Fielding had made her place comfortable and homey, with sofas and chairs arranged around the room, bright wallpaper, and a large rug that lay before the fireplace. A girl came in and served them tea. Ki took it gratefully and Jessie sipped at hers, her thoughts on James Campbell.

The landlady brought in her boarder and introduced him to Jessie and Ki as Mr. Justin Willis. She left the three of them alone, closing the tall double doors behind her.

Willis was a thin, bald man in his mid-forties. Thick wire-rimmed spectacles perched on his narrow nose and he walked with a bit of a stoop. He was dressed in a black suit, a tie knotted loosely around his cranelike neck. He peered at his two visitors through the spectacles. It was apparent that Willis was nervous and more than a little scared.

Jessie tried to relax him. "I'm sorry to barge in on you unannounced, Mr. Willis, but we learned you were planning to leave Las Cruces tomorrow and we had to talk to you before you left."

"Talk about what?" the skinny man asked.

Jessie said, "Why don't you sit down? We won't take much of your time."

Willis complied, sitting in a chair across from Jessie and Ki, his eyes glued to the rug in front of him. He clasped and unclasped his hands. "Why do you want to talk to me?"

117

She told him she had come to town to sell some cattle to Lowell Henry, explaining that she owned a ranch in West Texas. Without mentioning his name, she told Willis of Campbell's accusations. She mentioned that Ki knew the drummer, Horace Dunlop, who had said that Willis worked for Henry. She said, "I want to know if there is any truth to what I hear about Lowell Henry. Did he, in fact, knowingly sell spoiled meat to the reservation, and does he deal with the renegade Apaches, selling them guns and whiskey? If this is true, I intend to bring the territorial law here and make Henry face these charges."

"I wouldn't do that if I was you, Miss Starbuck," Willis croaked.

"Why?" she asked, seeing clearly that this man was one frightened soul.

"Because Mr. Henry isn't a man you want to cross. I tried to cross him. Word got back to him and he fired me. One of his boys suggested I leave town on the next stage or else I'd be in no fit shape to go anywhere. He has a lot of men on his payroll—tough men who don't mind doing a body some damage if Mr. Henry wants it done."

Jessie asked, "What did you do that made Henry angry?"

"Talked out of school, ma'am. I was mad, see, that I've never got any decent raise since I've been there—for a lot of years. I was out drinking one night and I guess I talked too much. I ran into that fellow Dunlop, the salesman, and he started asking me about Mr. Henry, and I told him everything I knew. He must have blabbed to somebody, or else there was one of Mr. Henry's spies at the saloon—I don't know. But a couple days later I got word that I don't have a job anymore. So here I am, waiting for the stage tomorrow."

"Where are you going to go?" Jessie wondered aloud.

Justin Willis shrugged his skinny shoulders. "Don't have no idea. Figure I might find work out in California. If I'm lucky. My luck's been pretty rotten lately."

118

Jessie was trying to feed her questions to him gently, gradually. She didn't want Willis to run out or clam up. She had to know what he knew about Henry's operations. So she started in again, trying to reassure Willis that she and Ki meant him no harm.

"Now, Mr. Willis, would you be able to repeat for us what you told Dunlop? It is very important that we know what illegalities Henry may be guilty of committing. As I said, the territorial law will be interested in prosecuting—if we can prove anything."

Behind the spectacles, Willis's eyes darted back and forth like a bird's. But he was reluctant to sing. Already, Lowell Henry had marked him as an undesirable. If the cattle trader ever found out that Willis had told these strangers what he knew, California might not be far enough to run.

"I don't know, ma'am. I'm afraid I've said too much already. I really better not talk to you no more." He rose to leave.

"Sit down, Mr. Willis," Jessie said in her best school-marmish tone. If gentle prodding wouldn't work with him, she'd try another method.

Willis obeyed. He seemed to shrink as he sat again. "I don't know." He shook his head sadly.

"What don't you know?" she asked.

"I don't know what will happen to me if I say any more. I'm scared, Miss Starbuck, and that's the truth."

Jessie felt sympathy for this man. He was caught up in affairs that were beyond his meager abilities. He was best at taking orders, not setting things right. She said, "I will see that you get the protection of the territorial authorities. You have nothing to fear, Mr. Willis. Now you must tell me what you know."

Willis gazed into Jessie's strong emerald eyes. He found no consolation in Ki's dark, Oriental stare. He was cornered. But at least this pair wasn't about to hurt him physically. That was what he was scared of most. He looked over to the door. No chance to make it over there before the strange-looking man collared him and flung him back.

"Well, I—" he began uncertainly. "I worked for Mr. Henry as a clerk. I toted up figures and wrote out letters for him. You know, a sort of secretary. I wasn't the only one. There were several other men who did the same job as me. So I did get to see a lot of what he did—but not all." Willis stared at the floor as he spoke.

"There were a few things—bad things—that I found out. I know for a fact that he wrote letters far and wide asking for men to work for him—men with guns. He paid top dollar for good help like that. And I guess he needed it."

"Why?" queried Jessie.

"Well, business—his business, at least—is dangerous in these parts, what with road agents and Injuns running loose everywhere. And he has made some enemies in town. He's got to protect his own behind—pardon, ma'am. I mean to say, he had plenty of need, from all I could see."

"How many of these men does he have on the payroll now?"

"Maybe six or seven. A couple were killed the other night. They didn't work directly for Mr. Henry. But word was they were out to get some Injun fellow that Mr. Henry didn't like. I don't know what the man ever did to Mr. Henry. But seems he got away, killed the boys who were gunning for him."

Jessie and Ki both knew who those men were. But they gave nothing away to Willis. Instead, Jessie asked point-blank, "Do these men do Henry's dirty work—like trading whiskey and supplies to the Apaches?"

The scarecrow-like Willis scratched the fringe of hair behind his ear. He shifted uncomfortably in his chair. "I suppose so, ma'am."

"Surely you can do more than suppose. Was there ever any correspondence, any bill of goods or unaccounted-for money—did you see anything like that which would prove such a trade goes on?"

"Never anything on paper, no," Willis said, gulping air as he spoke.

Her patience frayed, Jessie prodded him. "Well, what do you know, then?"

"I heard talk—lots of times. I was always in and out of Mr. Henry's office. Sometimes he met with these men—I didn't like their looks. More than a few times they talked about running wagonloads of stuff out to the desert. I pretended I didn't hear—didn't even sneak a glance at these gents, so I can't tell you what they look like."

"So Henry *is* trading illegally with the renegades?" Jessie asked.

"Yes, ma'am, he is," Willis admitted finally. "That's a fact." He looked as if he might add something, but he pulled up short.

Jessie went on, questioning him about Campbell's allegation that Henry had sold bad beef to the reservation up north. Willis said he knew Mr. Henry did a lot of deals with the Indian agent at the reservation—selling blankets and foodstuffs, sometimes mules and wagons. He was pretty sure it happened, but Willis was unable—or unwilling—to say for sure. He did add something this time, though, that made Jessie sit up straight and listen.

"Mr. Henry just has too many dealings with those Injuns—at the reservation and in the desert. Once I heard him brag about it. 'Those goddamned redskins will do anything I tell them. They don't know any better,' he said. Once I heard one of his gunnies ask Mr. Henry if he wanted to use the renegades to punish one of his enemies. 'Not this time,' Mr. Henry said. I heard him say it." He tossed the information out, eager to ingratiate himself with his visitors, hoping it was enough to send them away.

Instead, Jessie seized on it. This was the first time she had heard concrete testimony that Henry had direct dealings

121

with the roaming bands in the desert. It made her sick to think of that man ordering the Apaches to destroy his enemies—thus removing the blame from himself and attaching further crimes to the Indians.

"My God!" she uttered aloud. "Would you testify to that in a court of law, Mr. Willis?"

The former clerk started, clutching the arms of the chair with his bony hands. "I—I'd be mighty grateful not to have to, Miss Starbuck, I'll be honest with you."

Ki said, "Do you not want to see such a man brought to justice?"

"Sure, I want him to get what's coming to him. I just don't want to stick around to see it happen—maybe get mine first. I've got a ticket for tomorrow."

"We know, Mr. Willis," Jessie said. "It's up to you, to go or stay. But we need every piece of hard information you can give us concerning Henry. What else do you know?"

Willis went back to scratching his head. He wrinkled his brow and squinted hard. "Well now—I'm trying to think. Only that he's sending out a wagon tonight with his boys."

"A wagon? You mean to trade with the renegades?" Jessie couldn't be sure she understood what the man was saying.

"Yeah. Fellow named Jack Lansdale is the big tough in charge. Heard Mr. Henry tell him the day I got fired. I was waiting outside Mr. Henry's office when I heard them plan it. They didn't know I was there." Willis went pale as the words tumbled from his mouth. "God—if he finds out I told you—" His hand rose to his throat. "He'll kill me . . ."

"You don't have to worry," Jessie assured Willis. "Neither Ki nor I will say anything about this. Please don't think we would do anything to endanger you."

"I just can't help thinking," Justin Willis went on, "that if Mr. Henry was of a mind, he could stop me from leaving tomorrow. Stop me with a bullet in my back. And if he heard me telling you all this, my life wouldn't be worth a

122

damn. I just got to get on that stage tomorrow, ma'am."

"Nothing will happen to you, Mr. Willis. You have my word. Now you must tell us one more thing. You say the wagon goes out tonight. Do you know when, and where they will meet the Apaches?"

"Gee, I don't know—I never heard them say. I guess they have a regular spot and a regular time. I just never heard what it is. I'm sorry, Miss Starbuck, but that's really all I know about it."

"You have been very helpful, Mr. Willis. Thank you, and good luck." She shook his hand, as did Ki.

They left Willis sitting there in the parlor, gripping his chair, looking like a drained but redeemed man. Jessie hoped her promise to him would hold—she'd hate to see him get hurt tomorrow before boarding his stage for California.

•   •   •

Jessie and Ki returned to her hotel room and found James Campbell waiting there. "No one else knows I'm here," he told them.

Jessie had to smile. She was glad he was there, relieved that he was safe, happy to see him. She told him of the visit with Willis. "He claims there's a meeting tonight of Henry's traders and the renegade Apaches. But he didn't know where or when."

"We can assume," Ki put in, "that it will be in the same place as last time—not too far out of town. Where we found the sign when we rode in."

"And within an hour or two of when we found it. Say, between ten o'clock and midnight."

Jessie looked from one man to the other. "Then that's where we'll be tonight."

They were all in agreement about that. If they could break up the trade, expose Lowell Henry's role in it, they would be in a position to go to the law with evidence.

123

Jessie said, "I think we should wire the governor in Santa Fe. The sooner he gets word of this, the quicker he'll be able to act."

She found some paper and a pen in her saddlebag, along with a small bottle of ink. Then she sat down to compose the telegraph message.

TO THE OFFICE OF THE GOVERNOR,
GEN. LEW WALLACE,
SANTA FE, NEW MEXICO TERRITORY:
    REQUEST GOVERNOR'S IMMEDIATE ATTENTION TO POSSIBLE CRIMINAL ACTIVITY LAS CRUCES. HAVE DISCOVERED POSITIVE EVIDENCE MR. LOWELL HENRY INVOLVED IN TRADING WEAPONS AND SUPPLIES TO APACHE WAR PARTIES. FURTHER EVIDENCE OF OTHER CRIMES TO FOLLOW. PLEASE SEND REPLY TO UNDERSIGNED IN LAS CRUCES SOONEST.
                    RESPECTFULLY,
                    JESSICA STARBUCK

Jessie read the message aloud to Campbell and Ki. "I'm a bit too sure of myself, but I want to get his attention," she said. The two men agreed that she had said what she had to. "Ki," she said then, "I want you to go to the telegraph office and have them send this wire. Wait there for the reply. I have a feeling we'll hear from the governor before nightfall."

Ki said, "We must be ready to move tonight, whether we hear or not."

"James and I will plot our strategy, round up supplies and ammunition. As soon as you get word from Santa Fe, return here. If you don't have anything by nine o'clock, come back anyway."

Ki left Jessie and Campbell and went out into the scorching street. He located the telegraph office a block from the big old adobe church that overshadowed the town's central square.

He handed the message to the telegraph clerk—a fat, sleek young man with pale cheeks. The kid read the message through once and looked up at Ki suspiciously. Like everyone else in Las Cruces, he knew Lowell Henry was the most powerful man in town. If he sent this over the wires and Henry found out about it—he didn't like the next thought.

Seeing his dilemma, Ki produced a ten-dollar piece and slapped it on the counter. "I will wait here for the reply," he said.

The young man slid the coin into his pocket and said, "Sure, mister. I'll send it out right away." He sat at the telegraph key and rapped out the message, looking over at Ki a few times as he did so.

The samurai stood away from the counter, near a window that looked out onto the busy main street. He kept one eye on the telegraph operator and one eye on the people that moved outside the window. Ki was taking no chances. The bell in the church tolled three times.

*   *   *

Jessie had slipped out to pick up the supplies they needed—ammunition, some food—and returned by six o'clock. She and Campbell broke and checked their weapons, oiling them and wiping them clean with greasecloth, ensuring that no dust or grit would cause a malfunction or backfire. They worked silently, glancing occasionally at each other, not needing to speak. They knew what had to be done. They waited for Ki.

Finally, at eight o'clock, Ki came back. It was getting dark outside; the shadows in the street below her window were lengthening. The air was gradually cooling. By midnight it would be pleasant. Now, with the heat-haze still rising from the earth, it was hot and uncomfortable. But Ki's reappearance turned Jessie's thoughts from the temperature to the business at hand. Ki handed her the reply from Santa Fe.

TO MISS JESSICA STARBUCK,
LAS CRUCES, NEW MEXICO TERRITORY:
    MESSAGE RECEIVED. SENDING A MAN FROM U.S. MARSHAL'S OFFICE TO LAS CRUCES TO INVESTIGATE CHARGES. ADVISE YOU TAKE NO ACTION UNTIL LAW ARRIVES. DANGEROUS SITUATION FOR YOUNG LADY. REMEMBER YOUR FATHER FONDLY.
                                    YOUR SERVANT,
                                    GOV. LEW WALLACE

Jessie smiled. "I knew he'd help." She showed the telegraph message to Campbell. He frowned. "What are you thinking?" she asked him.

"'Advise you to take no action until law arrives.' If you go out tonight, you are violating his official advice. I don't want you in trouble, Jessie. Let me go. You stay here with Ki. I can break up the trade myself."

"Not on your life!" Jessie flared. "The governor doesn't have to know what I do on my own. Ki and I are both going out there to put a stop to this business. And neither you nor Lew Wallace is going to stop me."

"Don't be angry, Jessie," Ki interjected. "I was going to suggest the same thing—that you stay while Campbell and I ride out."

Jessie's jaw was set firmly. "We will not speak of it again," she said. "I'm going with you both. Now let's get ready." She finished preparing her weapons, her rifle and the converted .38 Colt, her favorite gun.

The Colt, as she handled it now, brought back many memories. Ordered by her father especially for her, converted from a .44 to handle the smaller .38-caliber bullets, it fit her hand like no other revolver she had ever carried. And it had saved her life many times. The special weapon was almost a part of her. A strange thing to say, but that was how she felt about it. She replaced it in the holster, which she had cleaned and oiled as well.

Ki prepared his weapons, too: the small, deadly *tanto* blade; a selection of *shuriken* throwing stars; and the bow he had used the other day, along with a supply of arrows. All were in readiness for tonight.

Campbell said, "We should not all go to the livery at once. One at a time, we will fetch our horses and meet at a point outside of town. We must not draw attention to ourselves. I'm already a marked man in this town."

For the half-breed it was a risk, keeping his fine animal stabled at the livery. But he had no choice if he wanted to be sure it was fed and watered.

Jessie agreed. She consulted her small pocket watch. "In another hour we should begin."

They settled on a meeting place from which they would ride, hoping that Henry's men and the Apaches would be at the spot they guessed. This was their only chance to catch the men redhanded and try to make them talk.

They endured yet more waiting, until it was time for one of them to start. Ki was the first. Jessie followed in a half hour, leaving Campbell to come last.

She retrieved her horse, saw that it was properly saddled, and rode out in the fast-cooling night. There were few stars. She guided her horse out of town and to the meeting place where Ki was. In another half hour, Campbell had joined them. They were about two miles from the site where they had discovered sign indicating the traders. It was all they had to go on, but it was enough.

Campbell's great stallion lifted its legs impatiently. It had been confined too long in the stable. The half-breed gave it some head and let it move freely, but finally reined it around to where Jessie and Ki were, near their own horses.

Campbell dismounted and led the stallion over.

"Did you have any trouble at the livery stable?" Jessie asked.

The big half-breed shook his head. "I think the man there knew who I was, but he didn't say anything. He had kept my horse safely. I saw no reason to speak to him, and he no reason to say anything to me." Behind Campbell's statement was the implication that the poor stablehand was scared shitless and that Campbell had done nothing to change the hand's mind.

Ki said, "It will not be safe in Las Cruces after tonight. Not for us."

"We should have Henry safely behind bars at this time tomorrow," Jessie said.

"It will not be so easy getting him there," Campbell cautioned.

Jessie snorted, "Well, we won't get him in jail by standing here." With that, she lifted her foot into the stirrup and swung aboard her patient roan. It felt so good to be back in the saddle after two days in town. This was where she belonged! She was eager to ride.

Ki mounted his gelding with the easy grace of an expert horseman. He, too, was anxious to force this confrontation with Henry's men and the Apaches. Although the three riders would most likely be outnumbered, they had the element of surprise on their side—an initial advantage that must be exploited before the enemy realized what was happening. The intruders would have to approach quietly and cautiously before attacking.

Smiling sadly to himself, Campbell admired Jessie's spunk. Nothing was going to stop this girl in her pursuit of what was right. Nothing except a bullet one day. He pushed the awful thought out of his mind as he mounted his big horse again. He vowed he would kill any man who harmed Jessie Starbuck—even at the cost of his own life.

★

Chapter 9

The three waited beneath the star-shot black sky. Jessie sat her horse erect and tense. They were fifty yards from the spot where they had seen the tracks the other night. A series of high rocks that cut up and out of the earth provided them with cover. No one spoke.

They could not be sure what to expect. They had only Willis's story to go on. It wasn't much, but Jessie felt in her gut that the frightened clerk was telling the truth. Besides, there was nothing else to go on. This was the one chance they would have to get to the bottom of the accusations against Henry. They'd have to tread carefully, try to capture one or more of the traders and make them talk.

Jessie looked around at her companions, Ki and Campbell. Both men gazed silently ahead. She could tell they were itching for the confrontation, for action. Not that they wanted violence—but these men preferred resolution to uncertainty, action to non-action. Given a problem such as the one they faced, they wanted to solve it.

The wind from the desert blew cold, and Jessie pulled her vest tighter around her. Here in New Mexico Territory the weather swung from extreme to extreme: from blistering heat in the day to frigid cold at night, especially in the desert. She missed the Circle Star ranch in Texas, where she was used to the regular, seasonal weather. But now she had to protect herself as best she could against the cold.

Ki's gelding sniffed something and snorted. Ki quieted the animal. Campbell and Jessie kept their own horses calm, as the animals' ears pricked up and they moved their heads to catch the scent on the air. Someone was out there, moving toward them.

Campbell said in a whisper, "It looks like we're not far wrong—someone is coming this way. We must be ready."

"It's probably the men from town," Ki commented. "The Apaches wouldn't make themselves so obvious."

Campbell agreed. "The Apaches will approach from downwind," he said.

"Are we safe here?" Jessie wondered, turning to peer into the darkness around her.

"For now," said the big half-breed. "As long as we remain in one place—and quiet."

They ceased talking and stood listening intently. *Keeping the horses calmed is one thing,* thought Jessie, *but what about us?* She felt a film of sweat in the palms of her hands and a tingling in her stomach—the familiar signs of impending conflict. She wasn't afraid, just eager—like the men—to get this business over with.

Then they all heard it—the creaking of ungreased wagon wheels. The sound came from the direction of town, and it was moving in their direction. Gradually it grew louder.

Well, whoever these men are, they're not too bright, Jessie mused. *Why would anybody drive out with ungreased wheels—announcing their presence to everybody in the*

130

neighborhood? It's not my problem, she reminded herself.

It took several more minutes before the three caught sight of the wagon. It lumbered into sight, groaning under its load, and stopped right at the spot where Jessie and the others had guessed it would. That was one sign in their favor, she knew.

Accompanying the wagon were two men on horseback. The wagon driver was sided by a fourth man who carried what looked to be a big shotgun. One of the riders was a tall, barrel-chested man who was smoking a cigar. The tip glowed like a beacon in the night. From where the three watchers sat their horses, these men were little more than shadows, but it was possible to count them all and to follow their movements. It was clear that the traders did not suspect they were being watched.

Campbell smoothed the neck of his big stallion, keeping the animal calm and quiet. It was a small achievement to escape detection by these men. He was worried about the renegades, whose trail sense was so much keener and who moved with skill and stealth in such deep darkness. Hugging the jutting boulders for cover and keeping still were all he and Jessie and Ki could do. It would have to be enough to fool the Indians. For if the renegades caught a whiff of their presence, it would be all over in a few seconds.

So the party waited. They watched as the wagon driver and his rider jumped from the wagon and began pacing around it, checking the load and stretching their legs. Then the two horsemen dismounted. The big man's cigar tip still glowed, and he said something to one of the men. Bits of conversation drifted across to Jessie and the others.

"The last time I'm taking this trip," one of them said.

"Hell, you get paid good, don't you? Quit complaining, Cal."

"Ain't complaining. Just that I don't like it—don't trust them redskins. They'll wise up one of these days. The money ain't worth it."

131

The tall man with the cigar stood next to the man who wanted to quit. "Just keep your ears open and your mouth shut. You'll get paid fine when we get back to town."

"Sure, Jack," the man said.

So the big man was Jack Lansdale—the one Willis had said was Henry's hired gun. This meeting was proving to be quite interesting, Jessie thought.

The traders carried on this banter for a while longer. Despite Lansdale's admonition, they liked to talk. One of them said, "Sure could use a drink."

Another replied, "Don't touch any of this rotgut. Stuff is pure poison."

"Them Indians must sure want to get drunk if'n they drink this cow piss. Hell, surprised more of 'em ain't blind." That got a few laughs.

Jessie didn't like any of this. She could understand now what Campbell was driving at. These men had no compunction about trading bad goods to the Apaches, probably extorting high prices in return, or at least asking big favors. It wasn't right, and the only ones it hurt were the Indians. These white men were proud of their cunning, their "horse sense," but it would come back to haunt them one day—sooner or later. Jessie found some satisfaction in the idea that they'd begin to pay tonight.

"Quiet, you bastards," said the leader, Lansdale. "You make enough noise to raise the dead."

The men fell silent. They, like Jessie and her companions, waited now for the renegades to ride in. The tension was palpable in the darkness as the desert wind cut across the landscape. Everything seemed frozen as more slow minutes passed.

Then, almost imperceptibly, the sound of horses' hooves on the rocky ground could be heard to the east. As if by magic, six Apaches appeared on their ponies. It was difficult at first to see them, so well did they blend into the night from which they came.

Jessie counted them—yes, there were six. That made ten men at the wagon. She didn't like those odds, but there was nothing she could do about it.

"Welcome!" It was Jack Lansdale talking. He walked over to the Indians, who remained mounted. "We have whiskey for you. Come taste the whiskey." He gestured for them to get down off their horses and join him for a drink.

One Apache, a small, skinny man, looked to be the leader of the party. He said something to Lansdale. Only one word was in English: "Whiskey."

"Yes, yes, you old thief," the white man said. "Plenty whiskey. Drink at your own risk. Ammunition, too. Bullets for your guns." He gestured with his big hands as he spoke, trying to make himself understood by the Indian.

The Apache seemed to understand what Lansdale was telling him—everything except the stupid jokes. But he would not dismount, nor would he let any of his warriors do so. He waited for Lansdale to show the merchandise.

Lansdale snapped his fingers and ordered one of his men to fetch a bottle of the rotgut, which he passed to the Apache. The Indian uncorked it, sniffed it, and sampled it. He spit the stuff out on the ground and said something to Lansdale— something angry.

Jessie turned to Campbell. "Should we move in?" she whispered.

He raised his hand to indicate that he wasn't quite ready. Ki was absorbed in the scene in front of them, but he was ready to go whenever Campbell gave the word.

Meanwhile, Lansdale obtained a sack of bullets from the wagon bed and showed them to the Apache leader. The mounted warrior examined the ammunition and called another of his men over to take a look. Each of the Indians carried a rifle—though they were of different makes and sizes. These were guns captured from dead white settlers or bought from these very traders.

Ki, his sharp eyes growing accustomed to the darkness,

133

studied the renegade party. He thought he recognized them from the desert battle of a few days ago. They were proud riders, distrustful of the men they were trading with. Perhaps they had been cheated before, for it seemed clear to the samurai that they were expecting to be cheated again. He wondered what compelled them to deal with Henry's men. He supposed they needed the supplies. And in return, what did they give? Probably whatever American money or gold they managed to steal—as well as their "services" when required. Either way, though, Ki figured they got the raw end of the deal, for they could only end up dead—from the bad whiskey or from other white men's bullets.

The Indians were inspecting the ammunition, talking among themselves. Lansdale's men hung about near the wagon. The man with the shotgun cradled his weapon in his arms; he would be ready, if necessary, to start blasting. The Indians were aware of this, of course, for they had their rifles near at hand. There was no trust between these two groups of men.

Campbell moved his horse closer to Jessie and signaled to Ki to do the same. He kept his gaze fixed firmly on the activity at the wagon. He, too, saw the man with the shotgun and didn't like the idea of riding into those twin barrels. He said to Jessie and Ki, "This isn't good. If we all show ourselves, we will all be killed. I have a plan."

Looking at him quizzically, Jessie said, "I hope it's not a foolish plan, James. I don't want you to get hurt."

Campbell ignored her words. "Ki, you and Jessie stay here, behind these rocks. I will ride toward them and you will cover me. I will try to talk to them—but I don't think they'll want to listen," he added wryly. "I'll draw their first fire and try to answer it. You two will open fire when you have to."

"No, James!" Jessie whispered fiercely. "That's suicide. You see that man with the scattergun? One blast from that, and—"

"He will not have time to use it," Campbell assured her.

"I can't believe that," she said.

Ki shook his head as well. "You can't do it alone," he said.

Campbell said, "We can't just start shooting. I'll provide a distraction. They won't know what the hell is going on at first. That will give us a chance. I don't plan to get killed. That's the way we're going to do it." He glanced over at the trading party. They were still talking. "And now is the time."

Jessie was torn. She didn't relish the idea of all of them riding into a firestorm of bullets, but neither did she want Campbell to make himself a sacrificial lamb. She knew he was a marvelous fighter—but against ten men? It was crazy. She was about to protest again, but Campbell silenced her.

"Trust me, Jessie," he said. "I will not be killed. You'd better provide good cover, though." There was no arguing with him. His mind was made up, Ki saw that as clearly as Jessie did. "Are we agreed?" Campbell asked.

"Yes," said Jessie, reluctantly.

Ki echoed her assent. He held his bow and unsheathed a war arrow.

Jessie's grip tightened on the Winchester .38-40 that lay across the front of her saddle. *Damn the half-breed's stubborn pride!* she wanted to shout. If he got himself shot . . . she couldn't bear the thought.

Campbell reined his magnificent horse around and moved away from them. He circled back around the rocks to their right. Ki and Jessie dismounted and took up their positions. Ki kept his open quiver at his side, with one arrow already nocked in the string of his bow. Jessie, her hands still sweating from the tension, held her rifle up, careful not to jack a cartridge into the chamber just yet—the sound would alert the unsuspecting traders and Apaches. Her heart thumped wildly in her chest. And she waited.

The tall half-breed kept his Spencer in its saddle scabbard

as he cleared the sheltering rocks and rode ahead into view.

The Indians saw him first. They stiffened, and their hands went to their weapons. The big man, Lansdale, turned and saw the approaching rider. He went for his iron, lifting it from the holster on his left thigh. The other white men were confused, and looked to their leader for guidance. The man with the shotgun raised it at Campbell.

James Campbell raised his hand. He swung his horse to the left, stopping about thirty yards from the wagon. He spoke something in Apache, addressing the Indians' leader but not taking his eyes from Lansdale. The Apache replied in a guttural tone. He held his hand up, too, signaling to his men to hold their fire.

"What the hell is this?" Lansdale growled.

Campbell said, "I have told my friends the Apaches that you are cheating them. I told them they are stupid to trade with the white bastards who want only to kill them with bad whiskey and diseased blankets."

"Why, you son of a bitch! Who the hell are you? You better get your ass out of here—now!" The tall white man was furious, stunned by the boldness of Campbell's act.

"I would advise you to do the same," Campbell said evenly.

"I'll take care of him, Jack," said the man with the scattergun. As he spoke he lifted the big twin-barreled gun and stepped away from the wagon. At this range he would pepper the air around Campbell with shot. He cocked the big gun.

Just then Ki unleashed an arrow, aiming carefully and releasing the bowstring with a twang. The shaft whipped silently through the darkness and penetrated the man's chest. With a strangled cry the man stumbled back, the gun discharging into the sky.

The shotgun's report echoed off the rocks, and everyone froze for an instant. Campbell sat his horse, exposed to fire, as if nothing had happened.

The Apache leader looked from Lansdale to Campbell. Lansdale, his mouth open, stared at the dead man, an arrow lodged deeply in his chest and blood seeping from the wound, the shotgun in the dust beside him. At first he did not know what to do, and the revolver hung in his hand at his side. Then he dove to the ground, scooping up the shotgun.

"You red bastards!" he shouted. He turned the big gun on the Apache party. With a deft movement he cocked the gun and aimed it, squeezing the trigger and emptying the second chamber. He blasted the Apache leader from his horse.

Campbell whipped his rifle from the saddle holster too late. He sent a slug into the dust beside Lansdale. He looked over and saw the proud Apache fall to the earth, his body riddled with lead, a gaping hole in his gut. The other Indians whirled around in confusion, pumping shots at the trading party.

The other two white men had found cover by now, and were returning fire. Campbell squeezed off another shot at Lansdale and missed, cursing.

It was a scene of utter confusion. The Apaches wheeled now, firing at the wagon, and galloped off into the night. They emptied their rifles into the air as they rode away, keening at the death of one of their own.

Meanwhile, Jessie had begun answering the traders' fire with her own, loosing lead at the wagon as fast as she could. She shouted to Campbell, "James! Find cover!" She feared that he was too easy a target.

The half-breed kicked his stallion into action. The horse streaked across the line of fire, bringing Campbell to within ten yards of the besieged wagon. He pumped off three rounds that bit into the wagon itself, but did no damage to the men beneath and behind it. Bullets buzzed around him—from Lansdale's revolver and the others' rifles—but he paid no attention. He wheeled his big animal around and sped for the shelter of the rocks.

Ki watched this with fascination. He fitted another war arrow in his bow and sent it arcing high. It fell behind the wagon, but it must have missed, for the two men back there continued their vicious fire. Ki wiped a trickle of perspiration from his eyes and watched Jessie as she placed her shots more carefully now. But they were inflicting no damage on the traders.

Campbell came around to their position and leaped from his horse, carrying his sturdy Spencer. "At least we drove away the Apaches," he said, as he took his place between Jessie and Ki.

"And you almost got yourself killed," Jessie breathed. She was overwhelmingly glad to have him beside her, unharmed.

Grunting, the half-breed lifted his weapon to his shoulder. He placed two shots beneath the wagon—with no luck. The three men there kept up a steady return fire. Lead whanged into the rock in front of Jessie and Campbell, spitting dust and shards in all directions.

The horses tied to the wagons were going crazy. They whickered and trumpeted in fear, jostling the wagon itself, threatening to pull it away. But somehow they remained in place. It looked as though the battle was turning into a standoff. Lansdale and his men were nowhere close to giving up under pressure from the opposing trio.

Campbell said to Ki, "We've got to move that wagon out of here—or else one of us has to circle around to pin them down from behind." A bullet sang past his ear as he spoke.

Ki thought for a moment. He wasn't getting results from his expertly handled bow. The others were stymied even with powerful rifles. There had to be a way to drive the enemy out from cover. Then the thought struck him. "I know a way," he said.

He slipped back away from the rock face, carrying his bow and quiver with him. Jessie glanced back to see what he was doing, but had to answer Lansdale's constant fire.

Ki went to work quickly. He tore two long strips of cloth from his shirt. Taking two arrows, he wrapped the cloth around each of the shafts, just below the sharp tips. Then he crabbed over to Jessie's horse. There he searched her saddlebag until he found what he wanted: a small bottle of horse liniment that was mostly alcohol.

Returning to the line where Jessie and Campbell were trading lead with the traders, Ki brought the bottle to the cloth-wrapped arrows and carefully poured the liquid over the cloth, letting it soak in thoroughly. He placed the bottle to one side and took up his position once again near his companions. "I hope this will do the job," he said to them.

Jessie was feeling tired and angry. Already she had reloaded her Winchester once, and now she had to do it again. She let Campbell keep up their side of the battle as she worked quickly to replace the bullets. She saw what Ki was up to, and was glad he had thought up the scheme—anything to shorten this fruitless confrontation. For a while she had thought the Apaches might turn back and ride in behind them, pinning the three between Lansdale's men and the renegades. But, thanks to Lansdale's stupid killing of the Apache, she had a feeling the Indians were angrier at him than at her men. The confusion had worked to her advantage so far. But now she wanted to bring this fight to an end. Ki's way was a good idea.

Campbell squeezed off three quick shots, keeping the traders locked behind the wagon. He then ducked down as an answering round crashed into the rock where his face had been. He watched Ki nock one of the arrows in the magnificent long bow. The samurai then took a sulfur match from a small metal canister and struck it against the rock face. The matchstick flared brightly in the thick darkness. Then Ki applied it to the cloth, which absorbed the flame and gave off a heavy black smoke. Quickly, Ki lifted the bow, pulled back the string, and released the arrow in a short, gentle arc.

It looked like a blue-hued shooting star as it fell from

the sky and landed in the wagon bed. Ki then nocked the second arrow, applied another match, and shot this one too, with deadly precision, into the wagon.

The three men there did not know at first what was happening. The arrows began smoking, and gradually the flame spread through the wagon bed. Jessie could see the first tongues licking upwards. She and Campbell held their fire for a while, watching to see what Lansdale and his men would do.

The decision was taken out of the men's hands. The two horses yoked to the wagon whinnied in surprise, smelling the fire. Nothing could restrain them now. They rose up on their hind legs, their front hooves clawing the air.

Jessie heard Lansdale shout, "Hold the goddamned horses!" But neither of his men made a move. The horses bucked and pulled, finally bolting. As they pulled the blazing wagon away, the wheels cut over the body of the dead trader with the arrow in his chest.

By this time the flames were leaping high, seven or eight feet into the air. The crazed horse team pulled the wagon around in a circle. The three men behind it scattered for cover. In their panic, they did not know where to run. The fire illuminated a bright circle, making them visible to Jessie and Campbell.

The half-breed took aim with his Spencer and fired, catching one of the men in the thigh. He went down screaming, but Campbell cut off his cry with another bullet in the head. The man hit the ground in an ugly heap.

Jessie scattered several shots, but was unable to nail either of the other two men. She saw Lansdale's figure scurrying for a nearby low-lying rock.

Meanwhile, the blazing wagon circled again, and then the horses galloped off along the trail, flames licking out wildly as the wagon disappeared into the night. The second man found cover about twenty feet to Lansdale's right, and he ducked to avoid a bullet before diving for shelter. Within a minute, both he and Lansdale were trading shots with Jessie and Campbell once again.

"We got one of them," Campbell muttered.

"Thanks, Ki," Jessie called over her shoulder.

Ki, knowing the battle was not yet over, took up his original position. He still had several arrows left, and he meant to put them to good use. He breathed in the heavy smoke from Campbell's and Jessie's guns. He, too, wanted to end the fight as quickly as possible, and now his side was closer to doing just that—if they could pick off one more man and compel the other to surrender.

But the big man called Lansdale gave no evidence of giving up. He kept up a blistering volley of gunfire, along with a series of shouted curses. He was angry, that much was clear. And his sole remaining crony did the best he could, gamely spraying the enemy line with lead. They weren't going to fold just yet.

Jessie's fury was mixed with a grudging respect for Lansdale. She wanted to keep him alive if possible. He would be the one to talk to about Henry's operations. But how to get to him? The only way was to wear both men down, hold them where they were until they ran out of ammunition or realized they had no chance of escape. She wondered where the two other horses were, Lansdale's and the other man's. If they made a run for the horses...no, she was confident that she or Campbell or Ki would cut them down if they tried such a bold move.

Her Winchester was hot to the touch. She wondered how long she had been firing it. It seemed like an eternity. Glancing over at Campbell, she saw him holding up, waiting for an answer from Lansdale. The answer wasn't long in coming—three quick rounds that ricocheted off the rock in front of them. They were lucky that the traders hadn't been better shots or in a better position.

But Jessie and Campbell blasted away at the enemy, Campbell taking Lansdale, Jessie the other man. She levered off two shots, paused, and waited to see if he would show himself before returning fire, then sent two more slugs at him. The man stayed low and did not betray his exact location, or expose any part of himself.

Meanwhile, Ki tried to get a fix on Lansdale's position, but it was difficult because of the darkness and because the man shot from slightly different spots as he responded to Campbell's attack. So the samurai bided his time rather than waste an arrow.

Seeing this stalemate, Campbell once again decided to take the offensive. He told his companions, "I'm going to try to outflank them. I'll go to the left. Cover me."

He had moved out before Jessie could say anything against it. She watched him go, peppering the ground in front of her with timed shots to keep the two traders occupied. Campbell slipped away into the darkness unseen.

Jessie continued scattering rounds like this for another minute or so. Then gunfire erupted to her left, among some rocks near the enemy position. Lansdale and his man turned their attention in that direction. But it turned out to be too late. Campbell had caught Lansdale's man unawares. The half-breed gut-shot the unsuspecting trader before he could get off more than a few rounds. The man took the burning bullet and bent in half and died.

Lansdale did not cease his angry fire, realizing now that he was caught in a surprise crossfire. Campbell took advantage, with punishing accuracy driving the big man back under cover.

Jessie shouted, "Are you all right?"

Campbell pumped one more shot at Lansdale for good measure and replied, "Yes. He's pinned down. I think we have this one."

"The hell you do!" bellowed Jack Lansdale. "You'll have to come and get me if you want me."

"Give up and we won't hurt you!" Jessie called to him.

"Who the hell is that?" Lansdale shouted, surprised to

hear the female voice laying down conditions for his surrender.

"My name is Jessica Starbuck. I know you are Jack Lansdale."

Silence greeted her statement. Lansdale didn't know what to make of it. Then, as if he had only one way of answering her, he opened fire once again on her position.

While she was talking, Ki had been listening for Lansdale to talk as well. This helped him gain a better idea as to the man's exact location. He had an arrow ready. He heard both Campbell and Jessie pin the man in their vicious crossfire. Taking aim into the dark sky, Ki shot the arrow in a very high, tight arc, gauging as best he could where it would come down. The arrow made its noiseless track against the stars.

"Goddamn!" came Lansdale's anguished cry. His gun clattered to the ground. He said nothing as Jessie and Campbell held their fire. "You sonsabitches," he cursed finally. "You can come on in and kill me. Oh Christ, that hurts!"

"Be careful, it might be a trap, Jessie," James Campbell called. He began to pick his way cautiously to where Lansdale lay. He held his carbine at the ready, capable of planting a bullet in the man's chest if this was a trick.

Ki and Jessie moved out too, traversing the open ground where three dead bodies—the Apache's and two of the traders'—were scattered grotesquely in pools of blood. They approached Lansdale's position slowly, carefully. Ki was almost a hundred percent sure, though, that he had hit his mark. He helped Jessie climb over the jagged rocks, the bow over his shoulder, his *tanto* blade in one hand.

Jack Lansdale lay on the ground, one big hand clutching an arrow embedded in his right shoulder. His face was contorted in pain and anger. He looked up and saw the two strange-looking men and one young woman standing over him.

"Who the hell *are* you people?" he demanded again. His craggy face was drained of blood and his shoulder was a mess with the arrow lodged there, but he wasn't cowed. His eyes blazed wildly in the darkness as he watched them move closer. He gripped the arrow's shaft in his hand as if he wanted to pull it out. "Jesus, it hurts!" he said again. "For God's sake, pull it out of me!"

Campbell stepped over to the downed man and scrutinized the shoulder, then said, "I reckon we'd better not do that. You might bleed to death, and we wouldn't want that to happen—at least not until you tell us what we want to know."

"You son of a bitch," Lansdale groaned. His face was soaked with sweat. He was a tall, powerfully built man, maybe forty years old, with thick gray hair. "Tell me who—" he gritted.

"I told you who I am," Jessie replied. "I'm Jessie Starbuck. Now suppose *you* tell *us* what you were doing out here tonight. Who were the men with you? Why were you selling those Apaches bad whiskey and bullets?"

The wounded man tried to take in her words. He looked at Campbell and Ki, then back at Jessie. "I don't care what you want to know, lady. None of your damned business who I ride with or who I do business with."

"It's against the law to trade with the renegades," Campbell said evenly.

"You look like a goddamned redskin yourself, mister," Lansdale grated. "What you said to them Injuns riled them bad. You're a fucking troublemaker, is what you are. I ain't about to tell you shit!"

Campbell reached out calmly and, taking the arrow shaft in one hand, gave it a slight twist. Lansdale let out a blood-curdling scream, and Jessie winced and turned her head away.

"Your choice," Campbell said. "I've got no qualms about seeing you bleed to death right here, and you'd better believe

I can make it plenty painful for you. Or we can take you back to Las Cruces and let a doctor take care of you, in which case you'll likely recover. Either way, you'll tell us what we want to know. I don't see that you're in much of a position to argue."

Jessie was aghast at the cruelty of the half-breed, but she understood where it came from. As for Lansdale, he didn't care how many Indians died from his bad whiskey, or how many settlers died from the bullets he sold to the Apaches; she couldn't feel sorry for him.

"I didn't mean them Apaches no harm, didn't want no trouble," Lansdale finally croaked.

"I don't want to hear your excuses, Lansdale. Do you work for Lowell Henry?" Campbell asked him.

"Yeah," the big man said. "I ain't done nothing wrong. Henry ain't done nothing wrong, neither. I was just looking to make some extra money, that's all. A little bit of bad whiskey. They actually like the stuff. And a few old bullets, most of them no good. Likely to backfire on those redskins. No harm done."

"Trading with the renegades is one thing," Jessie said. "Cheating them only makes it worse. Henry is behind this, isn't he? It's his whiskey and his ammunition you're peddling. Tell me what you know, Lansdale."

"How the hell do you know who I am, anyway? How did you know we'd be here tonight?"

"We're not stupid. We almost ran into you the other night. You came to the same place. That doesn't show much imagination on your part. Tell me if Henry is involved in this." She pressed her point hard, letting him know she meant business.

"Hell, he's behind every crooked deal in Las Cruces. Everybody knows that," Lansdale said, his breath coming in ragged gasps. He was hurt badly.

"And are you on his payroll?" she asked.

"Hell, yes. You think I'd do this without getting paid

for it, missy? Henry pays good, top dollar. Ask any of his men."

"And how many of those men are there?" she went on.

"You oughta know that. You know everything else." Lansdale rested his head on the hard ground. When he looked up at James Campbell, recognition dawned. "Now I know who you are," he muttered. "A couple of boys got into trouble the other night. It was you they were after. A goddamned half-breed."

Ki spoke up this time. "Watch your mouth. I would like to cut out that tongue very much." It was no idle threat. He had helped Campbell defeat the men who had bushwhacked the half-breed. He would like to show Lansdale how angry he was about that night.

Jessie said, "We have to get him back to town. Get him to a doctor and keep him out of sight."

Campbell and Ki lifted Lansdale and carried him to clearer ground. They found the two horses and helped the wounded man into his saddle. Campbell tied him in place and tied his hands together with a strong cord.

Ki gathered the scattered weapons and roped them together and fastened them on to the second horse. Jessie gathered their own mounts and joined Ki and Campbell in the saddle.

"There's still a lot you can tell us," she said to Lansdale.

They began the slow ride back to town, the five horses making their way along the trail. Soon they came across the burning remains of the wagon. The horse team was nowhere to be found; Jessie guessed the animals had freed themselves by crashing the flaming wagon against a boulder and then run off into the desert. She was glad they hadn't been hurt. Whiskey casks lay scattered and broken on the ground.

Lansdale said, "Hell, them Apaches wanted that goddamned firewater." He spat to one side and tried to sit up straight. The movement caused him great agony.

146

Jessie said, "And what did the Apaches do in return for the whiskey, Mr. Lansdale?"

"They paid me," the man gritted.

"How did they pay you?" Campbell asked.

"They did what they were told," the big man said.

★

Chapter 10

They found a doctor in Las Cruces, an old Mexican who had once treated James Campbell. He wasn't too happy at being rousted out at such an hour, but he did a good job on Lansdale. After sedating the big man with laudanum, he extracted the arrow and cauterized the wound, then bandaged it. He agreed to keep Lansdale there until morning— it wasn't likely in any case that the wounded gunslick would be in any condition to try to escape—when Campbell would come for him to take him to jail.

"That will be quite a scene," Jessie said as they were leaving the doctor's quarters.

"You are welcome to come along," said Campbell.

"I have to talk to Lowell Henry again," she replied. "There's some unfinished business between us." She paused, then said, "I'm not looking forward to seeing him."

The trio stabled their horses. Ki and Jessie returned to their hotel, Campbell to his room.

Jessie said to Ki, "I'll need you to come with me, friend."

"I wasn't going to let you go alone," the samurai said.

Jessie smiled to herself. At least she had Ki—she always had Ki. It was the only comforting thought she could muster at this hour. She still worried about James Campbell. After tonight, his life would be worth even less than it had been a few days ago. It was at least partly her own fault for encouraging him to fight her way. But, she told herself, however dangerous the course they had taken, they were on the side of right—and Henry was very close to being beaten and exposed.

Right now, though, she needed some sleep—badly. She and Ki reached their hotel and went to their separate rooms, Jessie collapsing almost immediately in her bed. She did not rise until she felt the first rays of the morning sun filtering through the window onto her face.

Later, after bathing and eating a bite, she joined Ki and the two of them went to Lowell Henry's office.

On their way over to the businessman's headquarters at the center of town, Jessie hoped Campbell was getting on all right, that he could get Lansdale to the local jailhouse without any complications. Once they had the big gunman behind bars, they were one step closer to pinning Lowell Henry to the wall. She wondered, too, how Henry would react to her this morning. She had the evidence now, everything that Justin Willis and Jack Lansdale had revealed. That reminded her—had Willis safely boarded the westbound stage as scheduled? She and Ki stopped by the stage office to find out. She was relieved to learn that the clerk was on his way to California. That was one person Jessie wouldn't have to worry about at this point.

Jessie and Ki were admitted to Henry's inner sanctum upon their arrival. He welcomed Jessie only a bit less enthusiastically than he had upon their first meeting, and he eyed Ki suspiciously. Jessie introduced the half-Japanese man as "my friend and partner."

Henry said wryly, "It is rare when partners are friends. My congratulations to you both."

The businessman took his seat behind the vast desk, Jessie in a comfortable chair facing him, while Ki stood at her side.

"Well," Henry began, "have you been considering my offer, Miss Starbuck?"

"In a way I have," she said.

His face took on a puzzled expression. "I'm not certain what you mean by that. I thought that was your purpose in coming here this morning—to close the deal. I need that beef, Miss Starbuck, and I'm sure you need the sale."

"I'd very much like to make the sale," Jessie agreed, "but I want to know a few things first. A few things about your operation here."

Henry gave an exasperated sigh. "We went over this the other day. I run a large business here, with many facets to it. But that need not concern you. I am prepared to pay a premium price for your product. That is all you need to know, Miss Starbuck."

"I think not," she persisted. What she now knew about Henry's true business interests was gnawing at her insides. But she had to be careful in revealing just what she knew. She decided to let Henry draw it out of her.

"Well, I am having a difficult time understanding just what you think," Henry said.

"Let me put it this way, Mr. Henry. Since arriving in Las Cruces I have heard some disturbing things about your business activities."

Henry smiled engagingly. "Any successful man will face rumors and jealousies. Whatever you heard must surely fall in that category. As I told you, I have done nothing I need be ashamed of. I am merely a good businessman—though I must at times deal with some men I would prefer not to

151

deal with. That, however, is a fact of life."

"Would you describe Jack Lansdale as a man you would prefer not to deal with?" she asked.

His eyebrows drew together and he frowned. His eyes darted from Jessie to Ki. He said, "What makes you ask that? I barely know Mr. Lansdale."

"That isn't what I've heard. I've also been given to understand that Lansdale is a hired gunman and that he trades whiskey and guns to the renegade Apaches in the desert."

"That is simply not true!" Henry was livid. "Where do you get your information?" His eyes blazed at her as he tried to figure what she was driving at. Then he said, "Did you speak to that clerk who was fired the other day—what's his name?"

"Mr. Justin Willis," Jessie said. "Oh yes, I spoke to him."

"Well, that explains it," said Henry, relaxing somewhat, folding his hands over his gut. "He was a disgruntled employee spreading rumors. Why he was dissatisfied with his situation, I am not at all sure. But consider the source, Miss Starbuck, and you'll see that I'm right when I say that such rumors have no basis in fact."

"That's what I believed, Mr. Henry. Until I checked into one of Willis's accusations."

"Which accusation is that?"

"That your man Jack Lansdale is trading with the Indians. You know, of course, that sale of weapons and whiskey to Indians is illegal. And if a man in your employ—"

"You cannot prove these wild accusations, Miss Starbuck! I must insist we talk about our cattle deal—or else this conversation is at an end."

Jessie could see that she was getting under Henry's skin. That was how she wanted it, yet she couldn't touch him off right yet. She saw that he was squirming—the mention of Lansdale had done that. Henry wasn't used to direct confrontation of this sort, that was apparent. And talk like this from a *woman!* That was unheard of!

She changed her tack, asking, "Do you know of a man named James Campbell?"

"No, never heard of him," Henry said.

"I think you have," she stated evenly.

Lowell Henry bolted to his feet, his fists planted on the desk. He leaned over toward Jessie and Ki. "What is your game, Miss Starbuck? You don't want to talk cattle. You are trying to anger me, to test me, to see how I react to these outrageous claims you are making—the product, I repeat, of vile rumors. Remember, you are speaking to a respected citizen of Las Cruces. Do not make accusations you are not prepared to prove in a court of law.

"And what do you know about what goes on here in Las Cruces or in the desert or anyplace else? You ride in from Texas with your strange friend here, and you talk cattle with me. That is fine. But when you begin sticking your nose in where it doesn't belong—that is *not* fine!" The veins at his temples bulged, but he tried hard to control his temper.

"I wouldn't think of bringing these things up if I didn't have solid proof," she said.

"What proof?"

"I have spoken not only to Mr. Willis, but to Lansdale as well. I met him last night. We exchanged words—among other things—for quite a while. He told me many things."

"What things?" Henry demanded through gritted teeth.

"The Apaches—it seems they often take orders from this office," she said.

"That's a lie!"

Ki stood erect, tensed, listening to this exchange. He kept his eyes on Lowell Henry at all times. At the slightest threat to Jessie he would spring into action. He could see that her words were having an effect on Henry—an unpleasant effect. Henry was boiling. Jessie knew far too much. Ki kept his mouth shut and watched Henry's every move. The man was on the defensive, and he was unaccustomed to that position.

Henry sat down again in his leather chair, his fists clenched so tightly that his knuckles were white. He shook his head. "I do not understand what you want," he muttered.

"Mr. Henry, I came to this town to sell you some cattle. On the way to Las Cruces, one of my Circle Star men was killed by a renegade war party. Ki and I and another friend— his name is James Two Wolves Campbell—survived the attack. It was from James Campbell that I first learned about you."

"What did you learn, Miss Starbuck?"

"According to Campbell, you sold tainted meat to the Comanche reservation in the north. That meat killed many people, including James Campbell's mother."

"That is a lie," repeated Henry.

"You switched good beef for the rotten stuff," she went on. "You cheated not only the Indians but the government. That is a crime, Mr. Henry."

"You have no proof, other than a half-breed's word." Henry stopped short, realizing what he had said.

"You do know who James Campbell is, then. What else do you know about him, besides that he is what you call a half-breed?"

Henry bluffed. "He has a bad reputation in these parts. That is not the point. You have no proof against me."

"Last night Jack Lansdale and three other men drove a wagon of whiskey and ammunition out to trade with an Apache war party. I was there; I saw them and heard them. Fortunately the deal never came off. Ki and James Campbell and I intervened." She paused to allow her words to sink in. "One Indian died, and three white men—three of *your* men. Lansdale lived. In fact, he is living in jail by now. He told us everything. He didn't want to talk but we persuaded him. He will be a powerful witness in court, Mr. Henry."

"What business is it of yours, Miss Starbuck?" Henry said, the color high in his face. Then he began to cool off some as he went on, "I see your game. You are a very clever young woman. And your—companion here, he must have done his work well, too." Henry smiled now, revealing his gleaming white teeth. He gestured magnanimously. "What do you really want? Ah, before you answer, let me tell you what you want. This is an elaborate smokescreen you have thrown up. You want me to pay you an exorbitant price for your precious Circle Star cattle—isn't that it?"

The well-tailored businessman now wore a smug smile. He had figured it out, he thought. She was trying to blackmail him. He could deal with her on those terms. That made sense to him.

But Jessie was hearing none of it. "I don't want or need your dirty money, Mr. Henry. I want to stop you from killing innocent people, and from dealing with those desert renegades. I'm going to bring you to justice."

Her face was flushed with determination. She looked over at Ki, who stood impassively, absorbing every word.

Henry laughed somewhat nervously. "Come now. I see through your game. You are a shrewd businesswoman—I must give you credit for that. But tell me, Miss Starbuck, what is your price? How much will you take for the two thousand head we talked about, with an option on three thousand more? I told you I'm willing to pay top dollar."

"And I told *you* I don't want your money," she said. "It is blood money." She rose and stood glaring down at Henry. "It would be easier for all of us if you talked to the law yourself, cleared up everything you are involved in. If you cooperate, perhaps they will be more lenient toward you."

Henry grinned widely. Apparently he saw something extremely funny in what she was saying. "I assure you, Miss Starbuck, I have no intention of talking to any 'law,' as you put it. I buy and sell judges and sheriffs. I have no fear of them. I am my own law here. I do as I please—and anyone who doesn't like it had better get out of my way. You are talking foolishly, for such a clever girl. I am willing to discuss our business proposition, but let's not talk any more of this—this fantasy of yours. Do you want to sell me cattle or don't you?"

"No, Mr. Henry, I do not."

"Then," he said, throwing up his hands in resignation, "we have nothing further to discuss."

"Mr. Henry," Jessie persisted, "isn't there any way I can persuade you to stop your illegal activities? Your trade with the Apaches is dangerous—for everyone. Four men were killed last night."

"Because you interfered," Henry stated contemptuously.

"Yes, and I'd do it again if I had to," Jessie said. "If you don't cease, the law is going to come down on you—hard. Unless somebody else stops you first."

"And who, may I ask, would be foolish enough to try to stop me?"

Jessie's emerald eyes burned into Henry's. "James Campbell will try. Ki will try. And I will try. We are not fools, Mr. Henry. You are the fool."

He laughed again. "You can't touch me. My men will cut you down before you can get close. I'd hate to see a pretty girl like you get hurt."

Ki took a step forward. "Do not threaten Miss Starbuck. You'll answer to me if you try to hurt her," he said, the menace in his voice unmistakable.

The businessman sensed that Ki was capable of killing him right here, and he back off. "I was only speaking of my men—they sometimes get carried away. I wouldn't want that to happen."

"If that happens—I will come after you," Ki promised him.

Henry growled, "You are both making a mistake. We could put together a good deal and you could be on your way today. There is no reason for you to meddle in my affairs."

"Ever since your men tried to kill James Campbell, I have been determined to get to the bottom of this. I'm beginning to wonder if those Apaches we ran into out in the desert weren't under your orders to attack anyone who got close to Las Cruces."

"Of course not, I—" Henry clammed up tight. He had been about to say something, but he caught himself in time. "I cannot imagine that—I mean, I have no control over what those renegades do."

He did not convince Jessie and Ki. "Well, the territorial law is coming to Las Cruces, Mr. Henry. There will be an investigation, and we shall see who is telling the truth," Jessie said. "The governor himself, General Wallace, has been informed of the charges against you. So you see, there's no escaping it."

"The governor?" he said incredulously. "Why? Why did you do this to me?"

"Why did you sell diseased meat to the reservation?" she replied.

"Goddamn you," he hissed. "Both of you—get out! Now! Before I lose my temper and do something I'll regret. I swear, you won't get away with this."

"You are the one who is not getting away, Mr. Henry," Jessie said as she turned to go. Ki followed her out of Henry's office. Henry came around from behind his desk and slammed the door after them. The clerks and secretaries in the outer office looked up at the noise and furtively watched Jessie and Ki leave.

Once out on the street, in the white glare of the sun, Jessie said to Ki, "I hope we didn't tell him too much. I don't want him to do anything stupid."

"He has already been stupid—and greedy," Ki replied. "He knows he is in trouble. I think he will not hurt anyone now. Not with Lansdale in jail."

"I hope you're right, Ki," she said with a sigh.

•　　•　　•

Early that night, after Jessie had visited with James Campbell and eaten supper with him, a man came to her hotel room. Ki, who watched her room from his, quickly came out to see who he was, fearing that Henry had sent a killer to eliminate Jessie. But the man turned out to be Deputy U.S. Marshal Layne Bosse, from Santa Fe.

Jessie let the deputy and Ki into her room. "I'm sure glad to see you," she told Bosse.

"The governor sent me down personal," Bosse said. "He said it was important. I want you to tell me what this is all about."

For the next half hour Jessie told her story, from Campbell's first appearance at their camp through her meeting with Henry this past afternoon, leaving nothing out except her deep personal feelings for James Two Wolves Campbell.

Bosse said, "You've got this man Jack Lansdale in jail? Then he'll be your strongest witness against Lowell Henry. But we've got to make sure Henry himself doesn't try to skip town before we can bring him to trial. Also, I need to talk to James Campbell. He can help me pin down the movements of these renegade Apaches. I'd like to talk to some of the Apaches too, if possible—but I'm sure it won't be easy."

The deputy marshal was a young man, tall, very slender, with a streak of gray in his black hair just above the right temple. He wore a big .45 Colt revolver in a beat-up holster, and a belt full of cartridges. He dressed simply, in trail clothes—an open-necked shirt and denim trousers—and there was nothing fancy or pretentious about him. He looked like a sincere, competent young lawman, which was a rare breed. His darting gray eyes took in Jessie's beauty and Ki's catlike intensity, and he seemed to like them both.

Jessie said, "Those Apaches aren't the talking kind. But they'll be plenty angry at Lowell Henry. One of his men killed one of theirs last night."

"Henry has lost face with the Indians," Ki added.

"That should work for us," Bosse said. "Can we go talk to Campbell now?"

158

Jessie, Ki, and the deputy marshal made their way across town. It was dark now. The quarter moon floated in the sky among the stars. The night had cooled quite a bit, and it was a relief from the steamy day.

Flores, the innkeeper at the Posada Dos Cuervos, recognized Ki from the night of the attack on Campbell. He appraised Jessie and Layne Bosse with a suspicious eye. They told him they were here to see James Campbell.

"Are they okay?" Flores asked Ki, his eyes narrowed.

"They are friends of Campbell, Señor Flores," Ki replied. "They are okay, indeed."

The innkeeper nodded. "You know where the room is," he told Ki. "Go on up. I must stay here to watch the door. I do not want any more killing in my *posada.*"

Ki nodded his thanks and led Jessie and Bosse upstairs. Jessie knocked on Campbell's door and said, "James? It's me, Jessie."

Campbell opened the door, revolver in hand. He hadn't let down his guard just because he heard her voice. He looked beyond her at Ki and Bosse. He let them in, closing the door behind them after a quick look up and down the hallway.

Jessie extended a hand to indicate the lawman. "James, this is Layne Bosse, a deputy U.S. marshal. The governor sent him from Santa Fe to help us."

Campbell shook Bosse's hand. "Welcome," he said simply.

Bosse outlined his purpose to Campbell, and asked, "Can you help me track down those renegades? I'd like to talk to them, if possible. I know it's not an easy job."

Campbell said, "They do not like to talk much. Not to white men—or to half-breeds. And if they do not want to be found, they cannot be found except by a long, patient search."

"Well," the deputy marshal said, "do you think it's worth a try?"

"They can't tell us any more than we already know," Campbell said. "We have Lansdale safely in jail. He should be enough to convict Henry."

Bosse stroked his chin pensively and looked at Jessie. "Can we rely on Jack Lansdale to testify against his boss? For a price, he might change his story in court."

Campbell got up and went to the small oil lamp that was burning by the window. He lifted the glass shade and lit a freshly rolled cigarette on the flame. Then he replaced the shade and walked over to Jessie.

She was saying, "He will talk. He has nothing to lose. And he probably knows more than anyone else about Henry's operation. We could even try to get Justin Willis, the clerk, to come back here to testify. But Lansdale alone should be enough to put Henry behind bars for a long time."

"I'm not so sure," said James Campbell. "Henry hasn't played his last card yet. Until he does—and until he loses—we do not have him. Lansdale is our only insurance right now. So we must be sure he lives to talk in court."

"You saying Henry might try to get rid of him, rather than pay him off?" Bosse said. He was not naïve, but neither was he as cynical as the half-breed about the system of justice in the territory.

"Henry cannot be trusted, it's as simple as that," said Jessie. "He's capable of anything. He ordered his men to kill James. He's been trading with the Apaches for a long time. He's been cheating the Indians and the government alike. Who knows how many men have been murdered at his word?" She was getting angrier as she spoke, remembering Henry's threats that day. "The sooner he joins Lansdale behind bars, the better."

Bosse said, "The best way to nail him would be to catch him in the act of committing some crime, or else make him confess. Neither one would be easy."

"He practically admitted to Jessie and me that he had done all these things," Ki put in. "But he would never confess. He is too proud, and too stupid. He thinks he is above the law."

Campbell looked directly at Jessie. She saw in his eyes that Ki had made his point for him. Campbell had never trusted the white man's law; that was why he had intended to kill Lowell Henry in the first place. But she—and his vision in the desert—had convinced him that he would be wrong to do so. She almost wished that she had allowed him to go ahead. If he had, it would have saved much bloodshed. And who else might now be killed before this was over? She shivered at the thought, feeling death very close at hand—right here in this room.

"There's no point in talking more," Campbell said. "You must arrest Henry," he told Bosse. "You are empowered to do it. The sooner the better."

"I agree," said Jessie.

The deputy marshal nodded. "I'll wire Santa Fe tomorrow. Territorial headquarters has to authorize an actual arrest."

"Do you think they will?" Jessie asked, concerned.

"From what you tell me, they have to. This man has to be stopped, the sooner the better, as Mr. Campbell says." He stood, ready to go.

James Campbell said, "Stay for a while. Have a drink." He produced a bottle of whiskey from under the table near his bed. He also had four glasses. "I told my friend Roberto Flores I was expecting company tonight," he explained. "Roberto provided me with the bottle and glasses." He smiled—for the first time in days, it seemed to Jessie.

She watched the tall, dark half-breed as he poured drinks all around. The four lifted their glasses in a silent salute. Jessie tasted a bit of the whiskey, and it burned all the way down her throat on its way to her stomach. She saw Campbell knock back a good swallow of the stuff.

Bosse allowed Campbell to refill his glass. Ki sipped at the whiskey with care.

The half-breed poured the golden liquid into his own glass and took another drink. Then he put the glass on the table near the oil lamp and stood there with the makings, rolling a cigarette. He licked it shut and put it to his lips. He bent down and lit it on the lamp flame, then replaced the glass shade.

Campbell stood by the window, smoking, and he picked up his whiskey glass. Behind him, the glass of the window shattered, splintering inward. A loud crack echoed from outside and Campbell spun halfway around, as if to see what was happening. A bullet had torn into his left shoulder and exited, leaving a gaping red wound. Then another gunshot sounded, and this time a slug ripped into the side of the half-breed's head, lifting a piece of his skull in a spray of pink and gray. Campbell fell to the floor, blood flooding crimson from his head.

"James!" Jessie screamed, and she ran to him.

There was a third shot, but no bullet came through the window.

Bosse, his revolver in hand, ran to the window and crouched there, peering into the darkness of the street, ready to answer the gunfire. But there was only silence now.

Ki was out the door, bounding down the stairs into the lobby. No sign of Flores. The front door was open. He rushed outside. There he saw the innkeeper hiding behind a post, his mouth open. He turned and saw Ki bolting toward him. He pointed to something out in the street. Ki looked and saw the crumpled body of a man, facedown in the dust.

"What happened? What did you see?" Ki demanded of Flores.

The frightened man, his finger frozen in the air as he pointed into the street, said, "That man—he shot—I saw him shoot up there—" Now he lifted a finger toward the window of Campbell's room.

"But he's dead," Ki said, incredulous. "Who shot him?"

Flores was shaking, barely able to speak. "Another man—

162

a shorter man—came up behind—shot him. I saw it. I ran out. Oh, *Madre de Dios!*" he cried, tears streaming down his weathered cheeks. "Did they shoot my friend? Did they shoot James?" he asked Ki.

The samurai nodded and ran out into the street, to the dead man. He hunkered down to inspect the body, then looked up and saw Bosse in the shattered window. He signaled to him to come down.

The lawman ran out into the street a moment later. Ki repeated Flores's story. He indicated a bullet wound at the back of the dead man's head, then turned the body over. There was an exit wound in the man's forehead. "Somebody stood behind this man, at close range, and killed him— after this man shot James Campbell."

Bosse squinted through the darkness, bending over to search the body. There was nothing—no papers, no money, nothing. "Who the hell—?"

Ki said, "I can guess. This man was one of Lowell Henry's hired guns. Henry sent him out to do away with Campbell. Then somebody silenced the murderer."

"Henry himself?" the deputy marshal said. "Is it possible?"

"Anything is possible. The innkeeper described the second man as short. That fits Henry. He's covering his tracks. He wants no one alive to testify against him."

"Incredible," said Bosse. Then his eyes lit up. "If Henry is out to eliminate everybody, what about Lansdale, the man in jail?" He stood upright. "I'll go there now. Only hope I'm not too late." He ran off toward the town square.

Ki had a sick feeling inside that Bosse was too late. He turned and went back into the *posada*, where he helped Flores to his chair, then went upstairs.

In Campbell's room, Jessie was on her knees beside James Campbell, cradling the big man in her arms, weeping. She had pulled a blanket from the bed to place beneath his shattered head. The blanket was already soaked with blood,

163

and there was blood all over the floor.

She looked up at Ki. "What happened? Who did this thing? They killed him. Oh, Ki—" She bent her head and tears fell on the silent, still form of the dead half-breed. Campbell's bloodstained face was serene, serious, peaceful. He would know no more grief.

Ki told her what he had discovered outside, then went on, "Henry has caught us by surprise. He has acted too quickly. He must have a plan of some kind."

"Damn him, and damn his plan," Jessie spat, her face drawn taut with sorrow and pain. She looked down at the man she held in her arms. Gently, Jessie laid Campbell down on the floor. But she could not take her eyes off him. She memorized every line in his dead face, traced the length of his body.

"Jessie," Ki said tenderly.

She remained kneeling by the half-breed's body for several minutes. Then, forcing herself to accept the fact that he was dead, she finally got to her feet.

Ki opened his arms and Jessie came to him. He held her tightly as she was racked by heavy sobs. He felt his shirt wet with her tears. The samurai stroked her golden hair, trying to comfort her. He knew, though, that nothing could pacify her—not now, with Campbell so brutally murdered. For a long time she clung to him, her oldest friend in the world. Ki just held her, let her cry.

Finally she pulled away from him. She looked into his dark, almond-shaped eyes. "Ki, if I had let James do what he wanted in the first place, Henry would be dead by now."

"So would James Campbell," Ki reminded her.

"Perhaps. But at least he would have got rid of that bastard. Oh, how could even Henry do such a thing? Ki, I don't understand—how can men kill each other like this? The way they killed my father—" Tears welled up again, and she swallowed hard. "And now this, now James."

"Do not despair, Jessie," Ki said quietly. "We will find Henry. He will pay for this."

"You're right about that," the woman said, her jaw set. She wiped her face on her sleeve. She would cry no more over James Campbell. Not until Lowell Henry had paid for his murder. "Yes, Henry will pay for this, Ki—he will pay with his own life!"

★

Chapter 11

Riding east into the desert, Jessie gazed into the distance, where the sun was just beginning to rise over the mountains. Washed pink and blue, the dawn sky beckoned her and her fellow riders, Ki and Deputy Marshal Layne Bosse. They were riding out after Lowell Henry.

Bosse had discovered, several hours earlier, that Jack Lansdale had been shot dead in his jail cell shortly after Campbell was killed. Bosse had then sought out Henry at his house, then at his office, only to find that the man had fled Las Cruces on horseback. One of Henry's servants had helped him saddle his horse and prepare a pack horse on which Henry loaded several heavy saddlebags. The servant thought the saddlebags must be filled with money—gold and greenbacks—and valuable papers. Henry had left shortly after midnight, giving him a five-hour jump on his pursuers.

The lawman had alerted Jessie and Ki, who immediately

joined him in the manhunt. After they took James Campbell's body to an undertaker, they went to their horses and saddled the animals. They made sure they had enough supplies—food, canteens of water, ammunition—for several days. They didn't know how long it would take to track Henry, though they figured they could catch up with him soon. After all, he was burdened with a pack horse and he wasn't used to the open trail—or to the punishing desert.

So the three of them rode into the great expanse of the White Sands Desert, the deputy marshal following Henry's tracks, which were easy to identify. Henry hadn't taken the time to cover his sign—another indication of his inexperience.

Yet, Jessie thought, they couldn't be too careful. Henry had killed two men within the past twelve hours, and he would not hesitate to kill again. She wondered what kind of weapon the businessman carried, and if he knew how to use it; probably he had taken a long-range rifle. Whether or not he knew much about guns, it was apparent that he would use one if he had to.

She felt consumed by anger and hatred. She missed James Two Wolves Campbell desperately. His death had left a hollowness in her. The injustice of his murder only proved the half-breed's original contention that the white man's justice was not meant to encompass anyone outside the system, such as himself. He had been prepared to die for what he believed in, but the way he had died—backshot by a hired killer—had been a cheat. He hadn't been allowed to fight back. It made her sick to think about it.

In her travels she had met many men, but none had touched her as deeply as this dark, intense half-breed. His sense of honor, his intelligence, his tenderness toward her— all these qualities added up to create a very unusual man. She wished her father had known Campbell, for, in a way, the two men had been very much alike: independent, strong, fearless. And she had loved them both, in different ways.

She remembered Campbell's vision when he had gone into this very desert looking for guidance, seeking to strengthen his medicine: the dead eagle clutching a dead snake. The half-breed had discovered that this battle was not for him to win—but did it have to end in his death? Campbell had known, or at least suspected, that it would. Jessie had not accepted that idea, and even now that acceptance was difficult for her.

Ki's gelding pulled up beside her. Ki could see that she was brooding over Campbell's death. He said, "We will find Henry. The lawman is a good tracker. Don't let it get you down, Jessie." He wanted to say more, but held back.

"I know, Ki. I can't help but think James should be with us right now. If anybody deserved a shot at Henry, it was James. And to think I talked him out of killing the bastard."

"He made that decision himself," Ki reminded her. "Besides, you did the right thing. If he had gone in and shot Henry, he would have been branded a murderer; he would have been disgraced."

"He died like a dog, Ki—shot by a hired bushwhacker. He was too good for that."

"His death will be avenged, we'll see to that."

Jessie hung her head. "I can't help thinking of his mother, and his mother's people, too—the ones Henry killed with his diseased beef. Henry deserves more than death. He deserves to suffer." Her rage was boiling over, and she said things she would not under different circumstances even think of.

Ahead, Bosse rode with his eyes down, following the tracks in the desert dust. The sun rose higher and the morning grew hotter. They had already traveled several miles from town. Ki and Jessie followed Bosse's lead. Ki watched both the trail and his friend, worried that Jessie would lapse into inattention; he could not let this happen.

"He is suffering already," the samurai said to her. "His guilt and his greed have made him suffer, and now he is

169

riding hard through the desert and it is getting hotter. He will suffer much more before this day is over."

"That won't bring James back," she said. She was lashing out, not against Ki, but against the unfairness of it all.

Ki understood this, and he said, "Nothing will bring James Campbell back, Jessie. You know that. We can only do what we have to do. Henry will learn the meaning of justice. It will be too late for him, but he will learn it. I promise you that."

She raised her lovely green eyes to him. "Thank you, Ki. I'm acting like a spoiled little girl. Perhaps I still am one. Even my father couldn't do anything about that." A faint smile crossed her dry lips.

"You are a strong woman," he said. "You will see this through and you will win. Our friend Campbell deserves no less."

"Oh, he deserves a lot more, Ki. A lot more than I can ever give him."

They rode on as the sun rose steadily into the white sky. In front of them and to either side, the desert stretched in the shimmering heat-haze like an expanse of bleached canvas. All of them kept their eyes peeled for any sign of the roving Apache bands like the one Jessie and Ki had encountered on their ride into Las Cruces. The odds were they would encounter some Indians, so they stayed doubly alert as they followed Henry's trail.

Henry had left in a big hurry, heading almost due east. He seemed to know where he was going, though as he rode deeper into the desert his trail grew more erratic, turning north at one point, then doubling back before turning east once more. Occasionally he zigzagged, possibly to throw off anyone in pursuit, but it didn't work. He just wasn't an experienced rider. Nothing seemed to deter him; he crossed high dunes and circled around jutting boulders, heading, it appeared, for the safety of the mountains to the northeast. But Jessie and the others doggedly followed the sign he left behind. They didn't know if they were gaining on him; they found no indication that he had stopped since fleeing Las Cruces. So they kept riding.

In the afternoon they stopped once to water the animals and to grab a quick meal of water and jerky. It was unappetizing, but their stomachs needed something. The water, though, tasted especially good. They drank sparingly, not wanting to waste a drop, for there would be no opportunity to refill their canteens until they found Henry, and maybe not even then. Jessie daydreamed of taking a cool, soapy bath, just to keep her mind off the intensity of the desert heat and dryness.

Bosse said, "We're getting deeper into renegade country. We're only ten miles north of the spot where you engaged the Apaches a few days ago. I haven't seen any sign of them, but they don't leave much to see. So we better be pretty careful, heads up and all that. No point in us getting massacred—that's not why we're out here."

Jessie had to smile. She liked Bosse. He was young and tough, and he had a no-nonsense attitude about his job. He wasn't puffed up over his status as deputy marshal. He was glad Santa Fe had sent Bosse out to help; he would get results if anybody could. Yet she couldn't feel as friendly toward him as she might under different circumstances. She could see that he was attracted to her, even though he kept his attitude and behavior strictly on a professional basis.

She wasn't after romance, though, and she doubted that she would be for a long time to come. There just wasn't room for that now. Campbell still possessed a big part of her.

"Ki, why don't you watch the backtrail?" Bosse suggested as he mounted his big bay. "We have to be catching up with Henry, though he shows no signs of slowing down. He must know where he's going—maybe to some renegade stronghold. After all, he did business with the Apaches, and maybe he thinks they owe him. If I was him, I wouldn't be so sure. But that may be his thinking."

Ki and Jessie mounted their horses. Jessie said, "I'm surprised we haven't run into any Apaches yet."

"We will, I'm pretty sure of that," the deputy marshal replied.

"We must find Henry first," Ki warned. "If he's fit to fight, he'll put up a battle. I don't want to waste any time fighting the renegades."

"We have to be ready, no matter who we come across first," said Bosse. "My guess is that we won't have much time between the two."

They rode out again, Ki taking up the rear, Jessie riding in the middle, Bosse out front.

Another two hours passed without sign of another human soul, without incident. By this time the sun was past its zenith, and now it slid down behind them, creating long, wavering shadows in front of them as they rode. Jessie felt the heat on her back and watched the stretched-out shadow of her horse as it ate up the desert miles. She took another sip from her canteen, her eyes never leaving the trail. They were deep into the desert now, committed in every way to pursuit of their quarry. And the farther they rode into the arid wasteland, the greater were their chances of meeting up with the renegade Apache warriors. At this point, Jessie thought she would almost welcome such a confrontation to relieve the tedium of the manhunt.

Ki came riding up from behind, pointing to the north. Jessie and the lawman halted and reined their horses around. There was movement about a mile off—several riders, apparently. The distant figures moved in a cloud of dust. Ki and the others watched for a moment, until it became clear that the riders were coming closer.

"Apaches?" Jessie wondered aloud.

"Looks like," said Bosse.

"What'll we do?" she asked, more than a little apprehensively. The last thing she wanted was another drawn-out battle with the renegades.

Ki looked around and spotted a stand of wiry ocotillo, the only thing approaching any sort of cover. "Over there," he said, and the others followed.

They dismounted, hitting the still-hot desert earth. Jessie held her .38-40 at the ready. The deputy marshal carried a .45 Winchester, along with his handgun. Ki, of course, strung his bow and took the *ebira* quiver from the saddle. They all watched as the distant riders came closer. They still could not count how many there were.

"They've spotted us by now—maybe a long time ago." Bosse spoke matter-of-factly, without a trace of fear or regret. "Do you have enough ammunition, Jessie?"

"Yes," she said. She had enough if the battle was short and decisive—but not enough to take her through a prolonged siege.

Ki nocked an arrow and crouched like a cat ready to spring, without moving a muscle.

Bosse said, "We'll have to open fire as soon as they come within range. I'd say thirty or forty yards. Otherwise we'll give them too much of an advantage. Damn, I wish I could see how many of those bastards there are."

Ki also was trying to count them. The party was just a dust cloud at half a mile. They were not moving very fast—which struck him as strange. If they intended to attack the small group, they should have been riding hell-for-leather at their target. Instead, they were taking their time about it. Perhaps it was a trick to put them off guard. The Apaches were clever fighters, always looking to put their enemies at a disadvantage.

Jessie, too, tried to count the oncoming renegades. She couldn't be sure, but she thought there were at least a dozen of them. Those weren't good odds, and as they rode closer, within the half-mile range, she felt the sweat on her palms that came when she was ready for battle. Whatever fear had been in her now melted away and she was ready to face whatever came. She lifted the long-barreled rifle to her shoulder.

Now the Apaches were within a hundred yards. Ki and Bosse counted ten mounted warriors. But there was something odd about the party. They did not wear paint, nor were their weapons drawn. Yet they were riding directly toward the threesome in the ocotillo stand.

Bosse said, "Let's hold our fire until we see what the hell they want. They don't look too unfriendly to me. I can't figure it."

Jessie, suspicious but somewhat reassured by the Indians' seeming lack of hostility, said, "Maybe they want to talk. I wish I spoke their language. They might be able to tell us where Henry is."

Watching the approaching war party, Ki noticed two riderless horses—one with a saddle, the other carrying saddlebags—tied to one Apache's mount. He pointed this out to Jessie and the deputy.

At about sixty yards the Apache riders halted, and one man dismounted. He was a young warrior who wore only a blue cloth tied around his forehead, and a loincloth and buckskin leggings. He was bare chested except for a bandolier slung over his left shoulder that crossed his bronzed torso. His face was as proud as his bearing—fearsome yet honest. He carried no rifle, but only a hunting knife in a beaded sheath tied to his leggings.

The young leader approached the three defenders. Together Jessie, Ki, and Bosse rose to their feet and, keeping their weapons at the ready, waited for the man to come closer. The warrior's eyes moved from one to the other, finally settling on Jessie. He regarded her curiously, but not savagely. He was unaccustomed to seeing a woman riding with men.

The deputy marshal raised his hand in greeting, signifying peace. If the Apache wanted to parley, that was fine—much better than fighting. Jessie's party was heavily outnumbered, and if they could avoid a pitched battle, it was to their advantage.

"I don't know their lingo," Bosse said. "But I'll talk if he wants to talk."

"I know the white man's talk," the young warrior said. And then, startlingly, he smiled. Seeing the surprised looks on the trio's faces, he gestured toward his comrades. "Peace," he said. "Not fight you, not enemies. This day we fight our enemy. He is there." The Apache leader pointed behind the line of warriors to the part of the desert from which they had just ridden.

"Who is this that you call your enemy?" Bosse asked, though it was obvious he already knew the answer.

"The white man named—" The Apache paused, apparently having some difficulty with the pronunciation. "Hen-ry. White man with two horses. He kill many of my brothers with bad whiskey. His men kill Eagle Claw, war chief. Now *he* will die."

Now Jessie spoke up. *"Will* die? He's not dead yet?"

Again the young Apache smiled. "Yes. When sun is gone, he will be dead." He gestured with one hand in an arc describing the path of the setting sun.

The members of the pursuit party glanced at one another. It was plain to all of them that Henry had met up with this band of Indians, and they had left him to die. A shudder passed through Jessie, in spite of her hatred of Henry; she had heard many stories of the Apaches' ingenious torture methods.

"We have to go get him," said Bosse to Jessie and Ki.

The warrior, however, was listening closely to what they were saying. His face grew dark and menacing. "No one help Henry now. He die."

Nodding, Bosse raised his hand again, saying, "We will not attempt to help the man, but we must talk to him if we can. Where is he?"

"Henry likes to talk. He talk to you. Too late for Henry. Even you not help him." The Apache leader was making a joke, for the others in his party grunted in approval.

Jessie asked, "Why did you trade with Henry in the first place? His whiskey was bad for your people. He could only do you harm."

"Eagle Claw wanted to deal with the white man. His warriors wanted whiskey. Eagle Claw was a great chief. We followed him. But now he is dead."

"Did Eagle Claw raid white settlements in payment to Henry?" she asked.

"Sometimes Eagle Claw killed Henry's enemies. He was happy to fight, even for the man Henry. I do not wish to fight for a white man—but against white men. I let you go free because you are enemies to Henry, like me."

"How do you know we are Henry's enemies?" Bosse asked, amazed at the Apache's shrewdness.

"Because you follow him in the hot sun. Only his enemies would ride after him into this desert." He smiled yet again, baring his teeth like a satisfied coyote. "We find him first. You can have him now."

"Thank you for allowing us to ride undisturbed," Jessie said. "I would like to be a friend to you. What is your name?"

"My name is Bright Sky in Summer. Tell me your name."

"Jessica Starbuck."

The Apache nodded. "I will be friend to the woman with hair like fire." With that, he turned and rejoined his men. He mounted his sturdy pony and shouted a command to his warriors. As a body they turned to the northeast and pounded off, taking Henry's two horses with them.

"What do you make of that?" Bosse mused as he watched them ride away.

"We still have our skin," Jessie said. "And I have a new friend."

"That's more than Lowell Henry has," said Ki. "We must be moving. We'd better find him quickly."

The three remounted their horses and set off in the direction from which the Apaches had ridden. They covered more than two miles, and there was no sign of Lowell Henry. They split up to search the immediate area, and agreed to regroup at the sound of a single gunshot from whoever discovered Henry.

Jessie skirted the edge of some low sandstone hills. Her animal picked its way among scattered rocks and occasional underbrush. It was only a couple of hours till sundown, and the dark shadows of the hills cooled her. She stopped to take a quick drink from her canteen. The water tasted delicious as it trickled down her throat. But it could not wash away the bitter bile she tasted when she thought of James Campbell's murderer. Even if Henry himself hadn't pulled that trigger, he had paid the killer—then cheated even him by snuffing him out from behind. Henry was a snake that had to be eliminated.

She badly wanted to avenge the memory of the handsome half-breed who had carried so much grief in his heart. She wanted to see Henry dead. But where was he? Then she heard a gunshot. She wheeled her horse around and rode toward the report on the double.

Bosse had found Lowell Henry. Jessie and Ki rode up to a tongue of desert sand surrounded on three sides by black rock and dry, stunted brush. Lowell Henry, the man who had wielded such power in Las Cruces, lay staked out, his wrists and ankles lashed to stakes driven into the earth. He was naked, his body sunburned to a purple hue and crisscrossed with deep cuts. Blood had soaked into the sand all around him. His open mouth was a black hole in his swollen face. Jessie wondered if he was dead.

But then he groaned and his eyes rolled open. He saw the three of them standing over him. His lips moved, but no sound came out. Ki bent to listen. Henry was asking for water.

Feeling sick to her stomach, Jessie turned her head away. "Cut him loose," she said. "Put a blanket or something over him. I can't stand to see him like that."

"We promised Bright Sky—" Bosse began.

"We can't leave him like this," she hissed angrily. As much as she hated him and wanted him to suffer, she couldn't let Henry die like this. Even she couldn't countenance the cruelty of such punishment.

Ki drew his *tanto* and sliced the leather straps that held Henry's wrists and ankles. Then the samurai went to his horse and removed a blanket that was rolled up behind the saddle's cantle. He brought the blanket to Henry and covered the injured man with it, according to Jessie's wish.

Henry only groaned in agony. He didn't have much fight left in him; his life was draining away quickly. He tried to keep his eyes open, but it was difficult as the lids were sunburned and swollen. Jessie bent over him and brought her canteen to his mouth. She let a few drops of water fall on his tongue. Then she poured in a small swallow, which he took greedily. His mouth was moist now, but there was not much else that could be said for the man; he had been badly exposed to the sun for hours, and probably had suffered internal injuries from the Apaches' expert beatings. As Bright Sky had said, he would die by sundown.

"Can you talk, Henry?" the lawman asked him.

Henry's lips moved. A croaking sound came out: "Yes— I can—talk."

Bosse showed him his badge and identified himself. "I came here to investigate charges that you have been selling weapons and whiskey to the renegades. It is also clear that you are involved in the murder of at least two men, having ordered the killing of a third." He paused, finding it difficult to look at the grotesquely suffering man. Then he went on, "What do you have to say for yourself, Henry?"

In answer to the lawman's question, Henry said, "I did it. God—damn—I did it. I'll go—to—hell—for it." He was hurting mightily. His face contorted and his eyes clamped shut as he let out a sickening groan.

Ki watched the scene impassively. Although he hated to

178

see any man suffer as Henry was suffering, he saw the justice in the situation. The Apaches had caught up with him and punished him more severely than any civilized court of law ever could. He thought of James Campbell and knew that even the half-breed—as much as he hated Lowell Henry—would feel a touch of sympathy for his enemy now.

Jessie squatted down beside Henry. She watched him for a long while. Then he opened his eyes again and saw her. "Should have—made the deal. I—pay—top price."

She understood the irony in his words, and she asked, "Why did you do it? Why did you have to hurt people, cheat the Apaches, kill James Campbell? You could have been a rich man still—the honest way."

"There is—no—honest way. I did what—I had to do." His breathing was shallow and he spoke almost in a whisper. He had no regrets.

Jessie shook her head. The hurt inside was almost too much to bear. But she no longer felt sorry for Lowell Henry. All along he had known what he was doing. And now he was paying the ultimate price for his deeds. It was as simple as that.

"We shouldn't let him suffer anymore," she said as she stood up. She looked to Bosse and then to Ki. They both agreed.

The deputy marshal said, "I'll do it."

Ki took Jessie's arm and led her a short distance away. Their backs were turned when they heard the crashing discharge from Bosse's revolver.

* * *

That night they rode back to Las Cruces with Henry's body. The next morning, Jessie and Ki saw that James Campbell was buried properly. Bosse wrote his report to Governor Wallace. Jessie stayed at Campbell's grave while Ki went to finish one last piece of business.

179

Ki found Rita in her room. She opened her door cautiously, but was glad to see it was him. She had her curtains drawn against the bright sunlight of midday. She wrapped her arms around him. "Ki, I am happy you came to me," she murmured.

The samurai embraced her, felt her heart beating beneath her breast. When she looked up at him with those large misty eyes, he wanted to take her. But first he sat her down and took his place beside her. She looked at him excitedly.

"Have you come to take me away with you?" she asked hopefully.

He drank in her sweet fragrance and gazed at her lovely face and lustrous black hair. "No, Rita, I have not."

Her eyes fell, but she did not begin to weep. She was a strong girl, growing stronger through this experience. Ki knew that she would be all right.

From his vest pocket he took the folded-up bank note that Horace Dunlop had given him for the girl. He handed it to her. "This is for you, from our friend Mr. Dunlop."

Rita took the note and read it. "Fifty dollars? For me? That is a lot of money, Ki. Why—why did he give this to me?"

"He is a good man. He wanted to help you get out of Las Cruces, perhaps go to California or someplace where you can find decent work, start a new life. He has great hopes for you."

"That was so kind of him," she said. "I did not know him well."

"He considers himself a friend of yours. He was helpful to me, as well." Ki went on to tell her what Dunlop had revealed to him and how it had helped to defeat Lowell Henry. He also told her about last night—how James Campbell had died, and how the Apaches had caught up with Henry. She listened to his story with grave fascination.

"It was so dangerous for you to fight Señor Henry," she breathed. "And those Apaches—they are bad hombres. I am glad you didn't get killed."

"So am I," Ki declared.

For the first time, Ki heard Rita laugh. It was a wonderful, musical sound. It was laughter stemming from sheer relief that the danger had passed and this man—who had shown her how to love—had survived. "Ki," she said, "you are a good man. I wish—" She didn't complete her thought.

"What do you wish?" Ki pressed. He wanted her to say what was on her mind and not be afraid of anything.

"I wish I was going with you and Señorita Jessie. I love you, Ki, and I want to be with you. Can you take me with you? Please, Ki..."

"I have told you, Rita, my life is committed to Jessie. Wherever she goes, I go. It is often a dangerous life, and I cannot make you a part of it. It would only cause you worry and grief."

Now the tears did come, but the girl kept her head up proudly. "I know that what you say is true," she choked. "But I pray that it does not have to be that way."

"So do I," Ki said simply.

Then she was in his arms, her lips searching for his. They met in a fiery kiss, and Ki took her in his arms and laid her carefully on the bed.

"Love me, Ki," she begged him.

He could not deny her, had no wish to deny her. She was so beautiful, so helpless, so sad, so willing. He removed her dress—she wore nothing underneath. Her lovely, heaving breasts were tender and electric under his tongue, and she writhed with anticipation as he took one nipple between his teeth. She tasted fresh and sensual, and Ki became almost drunk with the lushness of her. Rita put her hands around Ki's neck and held him to her, feeling his mouth on her creamy breasts. She didn't want him to leave her, so she pressed him more tightly to her.

Ki felt her hot breath, and knew that she needed him badly. He, too, had become painfully aroused; his groin was aching, his growing erection straining against his pants. He shifted so that he lay over her, and Rita helped him

181

unfasten and remove his jeans. He shucked his vest too, and was soon as naked as she.

Their bodies moved together, exchanging heat and need. Ki kissed her long and hard, giving her his tongue and tasting hers. The girl ran her hands down the samurai's naked back, along the spinal ridge, tracing the well-defined muscles and the sharp bones. Everything about him was fascinating to her, and she wanted to have him all, to touch him forever, to feel him inside her.

When, finally, Ki entered her, Rita gasped and clung to him even more tightly. For now, at least, he was her man, and nobody could take that away from her....

Later, though, Ki had to leave her. He went to find Jessie. She was not in her room at the hotel. He retraced his way through the sunblasted streets to the graveyard where he had left her. She was still there, standing over James Campbell's plot. A plain wooden marker stood over the grave. It was inscribed simply, *Here lies James Two Wolves Campbell, of two peoples. Let justice be done.*

Jessie's eyes were dry. She had long since collected herself and conquered the deep sorrow she felt. But she had not been able to leave the gravesite. Campbell still had a claim on her spirit.

Ki said, "Come, Jessie, we must go."

At first she did not move, then she looked up, her eyes meeting his. "Yes, it is time to go. Tomorrow we will leave Las Cruces. I don't ever want to come back."

They walked away from the place together. Ki touched her arm softly. "Your father would have been proud of you. You didn't give up. You stayed with the fight to the end."

"But at what cost, Ki?" Her question was a reproach to herself. "Still, we won. Didn't we?" Her green eyes flashed in the sunlight.

"Yes, we did," he replied.

Then she said, "You know, James and Don Schaeffer and all the others—they died for something. And we came awful close to dying ourselves." She spoke without bitterness, simply stating the facts.

"Let us bathe and have something to eat," said Ki.

"Good idea." She stopped and turned to him. "When we get back to the Circle Star, I'm going to ship a thousand head of cattle to the Comanche reservation where James's mother died. They can use the beef."

Ki said nothing, but she could tell he agreed with her. It was something James Campbell would have liked.

Jessie began walking again, beside her quiet companion. She felt cleaner now than she had felt in many days. She would be back at the Circle Star soon, and that was good.

Watch for

LONE STAR AND THE TEXAS GAMBLER

twenty-second novel in the exciting
LONE STAR
series from Jove

coming in June!

The hottest trio in Western history is riding your way in these giant

LONGARM adventures!

The Old West Will Never be the Same Again!!!

The matchless lawman LONGARM teams up with the fabulous duo Jessie and Ki of LONE STAR fame for exciting Western tales that are not to be missed!

__07386-5 LONGARM AND THE LONE STAR LEGEND $2.95

__07085-8 LONGARM AND THE LONE STAR VENGEANCE $2.95

__07611-2 LONGARM AND THE LONE STAR BOUNTY $2.95

Prices may be slightly higher in Canada.